HOLLY GASKIN

A novel

A Little Company

Outskirts Press, Inc.
Denver, Colorado

A Little Company

Outskirts Press
http://www.outskirtspress.com

ISBN-13: 978-1-4327-0579-4

Outskirts Press and the "OP" logo are trademarks belonging to
Outskirts Press, Inc.

Printed in the United States of America

This book is dedicated to two special people:

First and foremost, to my mother, Lillian Olmsted. She was a constant pillar of support and encouragement, and the greatest inspiration of my life.

And also to Pauline Galiza, a unique and wonderful lady.

I wish you both could have lived to see this book in print, but I know that you are together, watching me and smiling down proudly, in Heaven.

PROLOGUE

Pauline was ten when her father killed her mother. She tried not to think about that terrible day, or the day Walter died. There were few distractions, though, in her attic prison, so it took a great amount of willpower to keep from replaying the horrific scenes of last winter. But she knew she would go crazy if she thought about it. Pauline wasn't about to let that happen.

Instead, she passed the time by making up pleasant little stories in her head; weaving together fantasies with the few happy memories she had. On occasion, she'd converse with an invisible playmate, whom she imagined was sitting in the tree branches outside her window. Other times, Pauline would recite poems that she'd learned in school. Anything, to keep from remembering.

Sometimes, she plotted ways to break out of her dreary confines and run away from Poppa, but they all seemed too dangerous to try and carry out. She wasn't that brave. Even if she did manage to get away, Pauline knew she wouldn't get far. She had no money, not even a penny. Besides, even if she had enough money to buy a train ticket, a little girl traveling alone would attract attention. Adams was a small town, and she'd quickly be recognized and returned to Poppa. She knew all too well what the consequences would be.

Although more than enough time had passed for reality

to settle in her mind, there was still a part of Pauline that refused to believe what had happened; a tiny, but stubborn fraction of her brain refused to accept not only the past, but also what was happening now. It told her that there was still a possibility she might wake up tomorrow morning to find that it had all been a nightmare; the longest, worst one ever dreamt. But as one lonely day bled into another, that sliver of hope grew dimmer.

CHAPTER ONE

Poppa had always been a strict man, but whiskey turned him plain mean. At an early age, Pauline recognized the connection between the dark, strong-smelling stuff in the bottle, and her father's habit of hitting Mama. She learned to stay out of his way when his temper was close to blowing up. She could predict these rages with an uncanny accuracy, the way Grandpa Frasier had somehow been able to know when a bad storm was coming.

Some nights Poppa would drink a glass or two of whiskey on the rocks, and he'd remain eerily calm. He'd sit in his armchair, and look at the newspaper by the light of the kerosene lamp, leaving Mama, Pauline and her little brother Walter to their own devices.

Other times, he'd pull the heavy chair close to the window, next to the Philco radio that only he was allowed to touch. The volume would be kept as soft as a whisper, a disembodied voice telling Poppa secrets. Sometimes, if the President was speaking, Poppa would mutter things under his breath. Pauline wasn't sure whether he was commenting on the President's words, or if he thought the two of them were carrying on a conversation.

Lifting the glass to his lips, he'd stare out the window, without expression, into the night. Pauline always wondered what it was he saw. All there was out there was woods. There wasn't a neighbor closer than a mile away. But Poppa kept his gaze fixed like a night watchman, on the lookout for trespassers and burglars.

Of course, like most everyone else in those times, Pauline's family had nothing worth stealing. They only had such a big house because it had been left to them by Poppa's father, who'd died when Pauline was six and Walter was just two. Otherwise, they'd still be living in the two-room shack near the railroad tracks. She could still recall how the walls would shake whenever the train roared past. It had scared her when she was small, and she'd run crying to Mama, sure that the house was about to collapse on top of them.

Poppa had been one of four children. He was the oldest, and the only son. He had inherited "The Old Homestead" when Grandpa died. His three sisters divided up most of the household contents amongst themselves, leaving the place nearly empty. The few pieces of furniture they had now, Poppa had carted over from their old house.

In the living room, there was a rocking chair for Mama and an overstuffed armchair for Poppa, but no sofa. Pauline and Walter each had a wooden apple crate to sit on, which they made more comfortable by fashioning "cushions" out of burlap flour bags. The centerpiece of the room was the large fireplace, which the family relied on for heat during the frigid North Country winters.

In the kitchen, was a timeworn wooden table with uneven legs. It took up most of the space in the room. There was a chair to accommodate each member of the family at mealtimes, plus an extra one that was kept in the corner, for the rare occasion when they had a dinner guest. The kitchen also featured a gas stove, only a couple of years old, which Mama adored. She loved to cook, and had loathed the primitive, coal-burning stove she'd been forced to use at the shack. Poppa, who almost never gave compliments, declared Mama "one helluva cook." Although breakfast was often no more than bread with bacon fat for dipping, and dinner was usually some variant of vegetable stew, every meal Mama made was something to be savored to the last bite.

The house boasted five bedrooms, but the three upstairs went unused. Mama and Poppa slept in the larger first-floor room, and the children shared the other. Pauline loved her brother, but she felt she was getting too old to be sharing a bed with a *boy*. Besides, Walter's lungs were bad. He had been prone to Whooping Cough since he was a baby. Pauline always slept with her back facing him. Mama often said it was a "double miracle" that Walter had survived being sick so many times, and also that Pauline had never caught the dangerous illness from him.

There were only two electric appliances in the house: the icebox and Poppa's radio. Pauline's aunts had taken the modern, plug-in lamps with the fancy shades, so her family made do with kerosene lamps and candles.

One of Pauline's favorite rooms in the house was the bathroom, although she would never admit such a thing. When she soaked in the claw-foot bathtub, she felt like a princess. It was a great improvement over the ancient tin tub that Poppa used to lug out of the shed once a week, filling it with water from a rusty outdoor pump. There was even- wonder of wonders!- an actual, flushing toilet, as opposed to a smelly outhouse. Walter had been especially fascinated with this incredible contraption. Pauline could still see him flushing it over and over again, laughing as he made leaves, grass and clods of dirt swirl 'round and 'round, until they disappeared down the hole. The fun went on until Poppa had caught him, and beaten him soundly with his belt. That ended Walter's fascination with the porcelain "toy."

Pauline was confident that she knew her father better than anyone. She used this knowledge to her advantage. With every breath, she concentrated on pleasing him, or more importantly, on not making him angry. *"Children should be seen and not heard,"* Poppa believed, and so Pauline was always quiet. *"A woman's place is in the home,"* Poppa preached, although women had been allowed to vote for many years now. (Pauline had learned this fact in school, but knew better than to mention it in his presence.) Instead, she emulated Mama; learning to cook as well as any grown-up lady, helping to keep the house squeaky-clean, and mending the family's clothes with straight, perfect stitches. She went to bed on time, got good grades in school and read the Bible often. Being good was easy, she thought. Pauline couldn't understand why Mama and Walter couldn't learn to stay out of trouble by watching her and following her example. Somehow, they always wound up on the wrong side of Poppa's fists.

She tried not to look when he hit them, closing her eyes, or holding a book in front of her face while she silently cried into the pages. Often, though, Pauline couldn't help but peek, just for a second. That was as long as she could bear to look, but enough to ingrain the terrible scenes in her memory for the rest of her life.

Nowadays, she wouldn't allow herself to think about it during her waking hours, but the past haunted her in her dreams. The images were vivid and gruesome: Poppa's face, red with rage, and his eyes, glazed over with alcoholic insanity. Mama screaming, as Poppa pulled her by the hair onto the floor and kicked her, just because supper had been cold when he'd arrived home three hours later than usual. After such nightmares, she would wake up gasping, in a cold sweat.

Sometimes, she dreamed about Walter. In his short life,

her brother had suffered the worst of Poppa's blows. The whippings became an almost daily occurrence, but Pauline never got used to the sound of her brother's agonized cries. Poppa had seemed to hate the boy from the day he was born, perhaps because he was sick and weak. Pauline was sure Poppa had wanted a small version of himself, a strong boy who could hunt and chop firewood, and who'd grow into a sturdy man. But Walter was shy and easily frightened, and his skinny little arms would never be able to lift and swing a heavy ax. The idea of her frail little brother chopping down a tree was ludicrous. Things got worse every time Walter got sick. His coughing drove Poppa crazy. He'd turn the radio up. He'd pace. He'd drink. Then he'd come after Walter with the belt. Walter would try to run, but Poppa easily caught him. He'd beat Walter him until the boy was wailing, wheezing for his very breath. Mama would try to intervene, but then she'd get hit too. Pauline would remain quiet, invisible. She never let her fear show. Inside, though, her heart beat against her ribcage like a trapped animal.

The last winter they'd all spent in the house had been especially brutal. Snow blew in under the door. Outside, the drifts came halfway up the windows. Once, Pauline couldn't go to school for a whole week because the weather was so bad. Walter had never been to school at all, and Pauline spent much of that long week trying to teach him to read and write, and do simple addition. He seemed eager to learn.

The old Ford sat, useless, in the front yard for weeks. Its dark blue top was barely visible, peeking out above the snow. With the automobile buried to its roof, Poppa had no choice but to walk the two miles to his job at the lumber mill. He'd leave the house at 5AM, making the long trek in single-digit weather. Every day, Mama would ask the children to pray that their father made it safely to work and back. God must have heard them over the howling wind, for every night, around eight o'clock, Poppa came home, looking like a human snowman.

Pauline could still see Mama, rushing to help him out of his coat, saying how glad she was to see him, and thanking God for getting him home alive. She'd hand him a cup of hot coffee and tell him what delicious dish was being kept warm on the stove. Poppa rarely responded to all her fussing, and never drank more than a sip of the coffee. He'd stalk off to the bedroom, his legs moving stiffly from the cold, and change into dry clothes. When he came out, he'd help himself to a glass of whiskey before touching his supper. Pauline never heard him thank Mama for all the effort she put into preparing his dinner. In fact, he often grumbled that there wasn't more to eat. As soon as he finished his meal, Mama and Pauline would clear the table and wash the dishes.

On Fridays, Poppa almost always came home later than usual. Friday was payday, and as soon as his check was cashed, he liked to play cards with his friends. Sometimes, he'd be gone until Saturday morning. Poppa was very good at cards and hardly ever lost money when he gambled. Almost always, he would come out ahead. These were the only occasions when Poppa came home with a smile on his face. He'd walk through the door, pull a wad of dollar bills out of his pocket, and with a big grin, exclaim to Mama: "Let's ditch this ol' shanty and go buy that dream house, Mary!" Of course, Poppa was all talk. "The Old Homestead" would be their house forever.

One Saturday morning, a couple of summers ago, Poppa had come home with a carload of goodies for Mama and the children. The three of them had stood with their mouths agape as he hauled in armloads of items he'd bought in town, at the General Store. He lugged in big sacks of flour, sugar and cornmeal, which Mama promptly whisked into the kitchen. He'd even bought her a new apron, to replace the grease-stained one she'd been wearing forever, and some brand new Mason Jars.

For Pauline and Walter, Poppa had purchased a coloring book and a half-pound bag of penny candy for them to share. Mama usually didn't like them to have sweets, but she was so in shock at the sight of all of these gifts, she didn't protest as Walter and Pauline gorged themselves on gumdrops and taffy.

Of course, Poppa's winnings also paid for a large jug of whiskey and a tin of tobacco for himself. His eyes were gleaming like St. Nick's as he unloaded his booty onto the kitchen table. Christmas came in August that year.

Pauline often replayed that memory in her head, as she lay curled up on the lumpy mattress on the attic floor. It had been one of the happiest days of her life, and the only time she could remember all four of them laughing together. Now, days were long and dull. She slept a lot, out of sheer boredom, keeping her back to the window so the sunshine didn't keep her awake. Evening had become morning in her strange new world. That's when Poppa would come upstairs and unlock the door for her.

CHAPTER TWO

I n school, Pauline remembered reading about a remarkable girl named Helen Keller, who was blind and deaf, but learned to read, write and speak anyway. She liked pretending to be Helen. It was easier to close her eyes and see nothing at all, than to keep them open and see the holes in the walls, the dusty floor, and the dirty curtain that covered the small window. She wished she could be deaf as well. At times, she even picked bits of yellowed cotton out of the mattress and stuffed it in her ears, so she wouldn't hear the scuttling sounds of mice and rats in the walls.

Sometimes she'd hear the motor of an automobile, as it slowed down and parked in front of the house. Pauline learned to tell the difference between Poppa's car, the milkman's truck and the big truck that delivered ice in humungous blocks. Every time she heard one of them stop to make a delivery, Pauline would try to summon the nerve to scream as loud as she could, the moment she heard a knock at the door. But her voice seemed to disappear down a deep hole. She couldn't make a sound. Tears of frustration would well up in her eyes, because she knew that these were opportunities for her to be rescued, perhaps her only hope of escape.

In her mind, she played out fantastic scenes, straight out of the movies. She saw herself as the "damsel in distress," and envisioned her handsome rescuer, bravely sweeping her off her feet and carrying her out of harm's way. In the movies, the bad guy always got what he deserved. Real life, Pauline realized, was quite different. If she ever did manage to cry out, or make any kind of noise that led to her being discovered, her father would be furious. He'd storm up the stairs and bust the door down, with one violent kick. He would kill her with his bare hands, and probably do the same to the poor milkman or iceman, before they could even raise a finger to help her. And so, Pauline remained mute, her heart aching as she heard the vehicles drive away.

There were other sounds that Pauline couldn't ignore or block by stuffing her ears with cotton. They came to her in her dreams. That's when she heard Walter wailing, rapping on the windows, begging to be let into the house. She was haunted by the rhythmic pounding of his small fists on the front door. The knocking was frantic and forceful at first. Gradually, it grew weaker, as his strength waned. Walter yelled until his voice was hoarse. Ultimately, his demanding cries became sobs of resignation. Soon afterwards, there was nothing to be heard except for the howling wind.

Although this dream had many variations, one thing remained consistent: Pauline was always paralyzed in it. She'd be lying in some ridiculous place, such as on the kitchen table or in the middle of the floor. She couldn't move any part of her body below her neck. Her neck itself took on a swan-like quality. Pauline was able to stretch it at impossible angles, watching her little brother's face appear in *this* window, then in *that* window. Sometimes she'd see him pop up in more than one window at the same time. His familiar, normally mellow face was distorted with terror, and sometimes anger. Pauline wondered: was he mad at *her* for not coming to his rescue? Unable to speak, she'd mouth to him: *"I can't move! I'm paralyzed!"* but she had no voice to say the words out loud.

Like snowflakes, no two of her dreams were exactly the same. Sometimes all that was different was a tiny detail, like the color of Walter's scarf. Poppa was almost always present. Usually, he was laughing at Walter's predicament. Other times, he'd be reading his newspaper, while Mama stirred a pot in the kitchen, both of them acting as though nothing unusual was happening. Another time, Poppa turned the radio up to an ear-splitting volume to drown out the sound of Walter's knocking. The President's speech was battling with Big Band music on the same frequency. Once in awhile, Pauline would be the only person in the house, and she feared that both she and Walter had been abandoned, and left to die.

Every time she had this nightmare, Pauline would wake up choking on a scream. Once or twice, she hadn't been able to stop it, and a shriek actually escaped her lips. It was a good thing Poppa had been working at the time, Pauline thought. Otherwise, he would have come barreling up the stairs to teach her a lesson.

Sometimes, the dream was powerful enough to make her feel nauseous, but Pauline usually managed to choke down the bile that rose in her throat. Only once had she thrown up into the chamber pot. She'd been so ashamed of herself that it never happened again. Poppa never found out; She was careful of that. Otherwise, she would have never heard the end of his teasing.

Pauline's new method of fighting the queasy, after-dream feeling in her stomach, was to bury her face in her pillow and cry until her tears ran dry. She hated to be so weak, but crying took the focus away from her sour stomach. Lately, she found herself giving into her tears more and more, whether her tummy was upset or not. When this happened, she'd try and force herself to remember Walter during the rare times he wasn't sick. They'd shared many pleasant afternoons together; drawing and playing marbles indoors on rainy days. Sunny days were spent playing Cowboy & Indian in the woods behind the house.

One of her very favorite memories was a secret that only she and her little brother shared. Mama had been outside, hanging wet laundry on the clothesline. She usually kept a watchful eye on the children, but on that beautiful summer day, she'd been distracted by daydreams and hummingbirds. Like the stealthiest of cat burglars, Pauline and Walter had sneaked into the kitchen to steal the last piece of blueberry pie. It must have been a Saturday or a Sunday, because Poppa was home from work. He was snoring away in his armchair, and the children had to tiptoe past him to get to the kitchen. They'd eaten the pie in complete silence, with their bare hands, all the while casting furtive glances in Poppa's direction. When there was not a crumb left, Walter crept across the living room and left the empty pie tin on the floor next to Poppa's chair! Pauline had been both horrified at the naughtiness of his prank, and delighted at his bravery and ingenuity. Mama never did find out that *they*- not Poppa- had eaten the pie.

Memories like this helped her survive the long, dreary days. Still, Pauline wished she had a book to read; she was getting tired of making up stories of her own. She loathed the dismal, gray walls, and longed for some crayons and paper. What a difference it would make if she could draw a few colorful pictures to hang up. That would bring some cheer into the drab room. However, Pauline knew that even if she'd had an entire library of books to read, or the finest artwork to admire, she still wouldn't be able to avoid thinking of Mama and Walter. She missed them both so much, it felt as if a chunk of her heart had been dug out, and a cold stone put in its place.

Pauline also missed going to school. She'd been a good student, and she liked her teacher, Miss Webber, very much. Pauline longed for the company of her closest friends: Ruthie, Nancy and Mary-Rose. They'd been inseparable since kindergarten. Had they all forgotten her by now? The possibility saddened her beyond words. If she dwelled on it, she'd find herself fighting the urge to shed more tears, but sometimes she couldn't help it. Inwardly, she scolded herself for being such a baby. A ten-year-old girl was too big to cry. Or was she eleven now? Pauline had lost all track of time.

As far as the townsfolk were concerned, Mama had taken Pauline and run off with another man. Poppa had bragged to her how he'd fooled everybody, even the Pastor, with the story he fabricated. Pauline had been shocked that he'd lied to a *Pastor,* and right in the church! Wasn't that like lying to God Himself?

Without a wife and children in the house, Poppa could now have his rowdy friends over on Friday nights to play cards and drink. They were noisy, and their drunken laughter was audible to Pauline, even two floors above them. Pauline knew he told them the same story about how his wife had taken their daughter and run off with her boyfriend, probably crossing the border to Canada.

"They asked me why I don't try to find the two of yous," Poppa related to Pauline. "So I told 'em, 'I'm better off without the broad, and I never wanted kids anyway.' They sure got a kick out of that! Then I told 'em: 'I can do my own cookin' pretty good. Don't need to rely on no damn woman for that. And who says clothes need washin' anyway?' I tell ya, Little Girl, they about fell off their chairs! They were bustin' their buttons, they was laughin' so hard."

That was the closest Pauline had come to hating her father. She didn't have it in her heart to *truly* hate anybody, but it enraged her to know that Poppa was scandalizing Mama's name that way. Despite the abuse she'd endured for so many years, Mama had worshipped Poppa, and she'd tried hard to turn him into a good man. She didn't deserve to have her memory tarnished with ugly lies.

Pauline found a small amount of comfort in knowing Mama was in Heaven now, watching over her, but it wasn't the same as having her there, to hug and kiss her. She knew that Mama had believed in forgiveness, no matter what. Even though it was hard for her to understand how anyone could overlook Poppa's sins, Pauline tried to respect Mama's wishes by giving her father a chance to change his ways.

On weekday evenings, she'd listen for Poppa to come home from work. Not many automobiles passed their house. It was easy to recognize the rattle of the old Ford's motor. She learned that, on average, thirty-five seconds passed between the time Poppa swung the car door shut, and when he slammed the front door of the house. (*One buttercup, two buttercup,* she would count in her head to measure the seconds.) This would be followed by silence for ten minutes or so, while he had a swig of whiskey and took care of his bathroom needs. Then, Pauline would hear the sound of his heavy boots ascending the stairs. (Thirteen of them; she counted them every time.) Then, ten strides from the top of the stairs to the door of her room.

Her heart would beat in double-time as the rusty key turned in the lock. She wondered what would happen if that key ever got lost. Would Poppa even bother to try and get her out? Pauline shuddered to think that she might die in that room, slowly wasting away from starvation, all because Poppa had lost the key in a drunken stupor.

When they went downstairs, Poppa and Pauline hardly spoke to one another. They had become pantomimes, repeating the same routine night after night. He'd unlock the door for her, and retreat back down the stairs without even peeking in. Pauline would wait until he made it to the bottom to rise from her mattress. By that time, her heartbeat would be almost back to normal. She'd then get her chamber pot and bring it downstairs to dump out and clean.

In silence, Pauline would fix dinner for Poppa and herself. Usually, that meant a stew of potatoes and vegetables. Meat on the table was a rarity. Once in awhile, Poppa might shoot a rabbit or a goose, and Pauline would do the best she could with what culinary skills she'd learned by watching Mama. Once in awhile, something would come out too dry or too watery or a little burnt. The worst thing Poppa ever said about her mistakes was: "A starving man will eat anything that's put on his plate, even if it's his own shit."

Other than an occasional barb like that, father and daughter sat at opposite ends of the table and ate their meal without conversation. Afterwards, Pauline would go to the icebox and chip ice for his whiskey glass. She'd bring it to Poppa, who'd be waiting in his chair by the radio. He kept his bottle on the floor, beside the chair, and he'd reach for it as she approached. She held the glass steady while he poured. As he sipped his needed poison, Pauline would pack tobacco into Poppa's pipe for him to smoke later. She bet no other little girl had to do such things.

Dishes got washed, but not clothes. Poppa didn't care

much about cleanliness, and Pauline certainly couldn't wash either of her dresses, for someone might see them drying on the clothesline and know she was there. She bathed occasionally, but then she had to get back into her threadbare, unwashed dress. No matter how thoroughly she scrubbed herself when she took a bath, she never felt clean.

CHAPTER THREE

"**H**ere," Poppa said one evening, making her jump. She'd just finished washing a sink full of dishes, and hadn't even heard him come up behind her.

"Yes, Poppa?" Pauline wiped her wet hands on the skirt of her dress and looked up apprehensively.

He handed her what she thought at first was a curtain or a tablecloth. Pauline took it, looking at it without comprehension.

"That dress is getting too small for you," he said. "Wear this."

Pauline knew she had grown. The hem of her dress fell inches above her knees now, and the once-puffy sleeves had become tight and uncomfortable around her shoulders. She examined the garment that Poppa had shoved into her hands. Had he actually gone into a store and bought a girl's dress for her?

When she realized what it was, she nearly dropped it. She quickly recovered her senses and gripped it tight to herself, stifling her emotions.

The dress had been Mama's!

Pauline shuddered inside at the idea of wearing her dead mother's dress, even though this was one that Mama had hardly used. It had been a second-hand gift from someone in the church. Mama had worn it once or twice, to be polite, but she'd confided to Pauline that she thought its dark maroon color didn't become her. She'd stashed it away somewhere; Pauline had forgotten all about it until now. Although she couldn't pinpoint the reason, putting on the dress was the last thing Pauline wanted to do.

What's wrong with me? she asked herself. Having Mama's dress to wear ought to be a comfort to her. Holding it in her hands now, however, she feared that memories-good and bad- would overwhelm her every time she put it on. Pauline knew that her imagination must be running wild, but she thought that the dress even *smelled* like Mama, which was impossible after all this time.

"Put it on," Poppa said again. This time his tone of voice told her that it was a command, not a suggestion.

Pauline obediently went into the bathroom and changed. There was no mirror in which to judge her reflection, but she was sure she looked perfectly ridiculous. Mama's dress was too big on her. Mama had been a slim, petite woman, and Pauline had grown nearly two inches since last year. Still, the long sleeves came almost to her fingertips and the skirt fell halfway down her calves. Pauline felt foolish, like a little girl playing dress-up. Maybe Poppa would let her tailor it, to better suit her still-tomboyish figure. She might even be able change the buttons, or sew on a pretty sash. Anything, to make it *not* look like Mama's dress anymore.

Clutching her ragged old outfit, Pauline timidly emerged from the bathroom. She stood still, waiting for Poppa's approval. She stared down at her feet, nervously twisting the old dress in her hands. She could feel his eyes crawling all over her like a pair of curious spiders. He studied her in silence for a long time.

"You might as well use your old one for rags," he finally said. "It ain't good for wearin' no more." With that, he walked away, poured himself a glass of whiskey- minus the ice- and swigged it down in one big gulp.

Pauline stood still for almost a full minute before slipping out of the room. She intended to head up the attic stairs, which were to her right. Instead, she stopped in her tracks. Something compelled her to turn left, in the direction of the bedroom she'd once shared with her brother. She hadn't been in there since Mama died.

The door was partially ajar, and she pushed it all the way open. The full moon shone through the curtainless window, illuminating the bed and its rusty metal frame. Against the wall, stood the dresser that she and Walter used to share. The top drawer had been exclusively reserved for her "delicate underthings" and she slid it open now. She was pleased to find two pairs of clean, white underpants, which she removed to bring upstairs with her.

Next, she turned towards the far corner of the room. The wooden trunk, where Pauline and Walter had kept the few toys that they owned, was still there. She went to it and kneeled beside it, regarding it with reverence. A thick layer of dust blanketed the top, and she wiped it off with the old dress she was still hanging on to. Even though it had only been a matter of months since she'd last touched it, she felt like she was about to unearth a treasure chest hundreds of years old. She hesitated for just a second, listening for Poppa, before lifting the squeaky lid.

Pauline took each item out, holding them up to examine them in the moonlight. She found Sally, the doll she'd had since she was a toddler. The chubby-cheeked baby doll had been a gift from Santa Claus. Sally had blue eyes that opened when she stood up and shut when she was "sleeping." Three or four years ago, Walter had torn Sally's eyelashes off, in an uncharacteristic act of malice. Pauline had gotten so mad at him! That was the only time she ever slugged her brother. But she never tattled to their parents, because she didn't want him to get an extra beating from Poppa.

Pauline put the doll down and delved back into the trunk. She dismissed the half-dozen storybooks whose pages she'd worn out. They were all baby books, for children just learning to read. All of the good books she'd read most recently- great stories about pioneer children and even one about a girl detective- had been borrowed from the library. Next, she found the old tin whistle she and her brother had discovered alongside the road on their way to school one day. There was the cigar box in which they'd stored their marbles and jacks. Walter's prized toy fire truck was in the trunk too, but Pauline didn't touch it, out of respect. Her brother had never allowed her to touch it while he was alive, so she wouldn't do so now. She found a box of worn-down Crayola crayons (with the red one missing) and a pad of drawing paper. Pauline flipped through it, remembering when she and her brother had created each picture. They'd sketched trees and houses, dogs and horses, and some very unflattering portraits of one another. Not one page, front nor back, had been left blank.

At the bottom of the trunk, Pauline found Mark. She smiled as she lifted him out.

"Hello, Mark," she whispered. "I'd forgotten all about you."

Mark was a tin soldier that Walter had found in the woods during an afternoon of exploring. He wasn't really a toy, per se. Mark was more like the tin equivalent of a paper doll; flat and one-dimensional. He had a small dent in his chest, apparently from a BB gun. Poppa had told them that the soldier had been made especially for target practice.

"I'll be! You found yourself a genuine Marx!" he'd

exclaimed, referring to the manufacturer. But young Walter had misunderstood and thought "Mark" was the soldier's name. And so it was, from that moment on.

Pauline put all of the items neatly back in the trunk. All except Mark, whom she clutched in her hand- along with her recovered underwear- as she returned to her room in the attic. She tucked him under her pillow after she'd laid down. She felt a little better, having a part of her brother with her. She curled up under the thin, itchy sheet and closed her eyes. Soon Poppa would come upstairs to lock the door. With a yawn, she drifted off to sleep.

CHAPTER FOUR

That night, Pauline had a strange dream. She was in the yard of their old shack, sitting on a blanket that was spread out, picnic-style, on the grass. She was wearing her pretty Sunday dress, having a tea party with Sally. The baby doll, clad in a frock that matched Pauline's, had miraculously grown her eyelashes back. Even her blonde locks seemed to have grown longer. Tiny cups and saucers, painted with pink roses, were carefully spaced apart at four place settings. Sally indicated with an impatient hand gesture that she wanted her tea poured, but Pauline admonished her that the polite thing to do was wait until their guests had arrived.

All at once, the earth started to shake. The delicate teacups rattled against the saucers, and Pauline scrambled to keep them from shattering. She looked over her left shoulder to see what was causing this disturbance, and couldn't believe her eyes.

Mark, in his Infantry Private uniform, was driving a military tank almost as big as their house. He was still a toy, but the soldier was now life-sized and alive. Walter was perched on the seat beside him, a proud grin on his face. They saluted her in perfect unison as they rolled by, flattening bushes and saplings at the side of the road. Mama emerged from the house, a distraught expression on her face. She was wearing the maroon dress that Poppa had just given to Pauline. She ran after the tank, waving a cast iron pan in the air.

"Get down from there, Walter!" she cried. "You're going to fall off and get yourself killed!"

Pauline woke up. Through puffy eyes, she could see that the sky was just starting to turn light. She took Mark out from under her pillow and scowled at him.

"I thought you'd stand guard and keep my bad dreams away," Pauline scolded him. "Some soldier you are!"

She tossed him aside and sighed as she stretched out on the mattress. She was so tired of staring at the same ceiling and the same walls every day. She was running out of games to play to keep her mind from replaying the horrors of the past and worries about her future. More and more, she had been talking to herself. She was even growing weary of the sound of her own voice. Plain old boredom was one thing, but the loneliness was even worse.

Although she was still miffed at Mark, she crawled over to the spot where he'd landed, picked him up and brought him back to her mattress. He looked like the sort of person who could honor a promise and keep a secret. Could Mark be a friend to her now, as Sally had been when she was younger? She supposed that it was better than having no one to talk to at all. And as strange as it was to talk to a doll at her age, Pauline reasoned, it wasn't as crazy as talking to herself.

"You've been by yourself a long time, too," she mumbled to Mark, a little embarrassed at talking to a painted piece of tin. "You should know how I feel. I'd give anything to have a little company. I'm so lonely. I wish Poppa would let just one of my friends visit me, just once. Everyone thinks I moved away. But he could say I came back for a visit, that Mama let me take the train all by myself. Poppa's good at making up stories."

Even as she said this, Pauline knew this would never happen. She would never even dare to ask.

"Maybe I could ask for a little kitten," she continued, feeling more comfortable as the words tumbled out. "I've never had a pet. I think I'd be good at taking care of it. Even a bird would be nice, like a canary. My friend Ruthie Sullivan had a canary named Willie. He was a good bird. I think one of her little sisters left the cage open, though, and Willie flew away."

Pauline stopped talking when she heard a scuffling noise coming from the wall. Cringing, she rolled onto her side, facing the direction of the sound. She had a pretty good idea what she was contending with. From time to time, she would see an icky rat or mouse poke its mangy head out of a hole in the wall. She'd tried plugging the holes with rags and old newspaper, but the pests would chew through everything with their sharp little teeth, and drag it off to build their nests. She'd been trying to summon up the nerve to approach Poppa and ask him to buy some mouse traps for her room. It sounded like there were more creatures than ever. Either they were inviting their friends to move in, or they were having babies.

In the dim light of dawn, Pauline observed a shadowy movement on the floor. She squinted, struggling to focus her sleepy eyes. When she saw what it was, her skin crawled.

It was no itty bitty mouse she'd heard. There, no more than ten feet away from her head, stood a large rat. And *stood* was the right word, because the disgusting thing was up on his two hind legs. He reminded Pauline of a prairie dog, except prairie dogs were cute, and rats were dirty and ugly.

"I don't have any cheese for you. Go away!" she

ordered.

The rat just stood there, staring. Pauline pulled the sheet tighter around her body. Curling up in a fetal position, she tried to swaddle herself in the material, so that none of her skin was left exposed. She was worried that the rat might make a run for her. Did rats pounce? She didn't know for sure. Her mattress was on the floor, with no actual bed underneath. The animal would have no problem scaling those few inches to get to her. She couldn't stand the thought of its nasty little paws on her skin. She imagined him coming back while she was asleep, crawling beneath the sheet to bite her toes. She shuddered, thinking about it.

The rat got down on all fours. He regarded her almost thoughtfully. He seemed to be trying to decide whether she was a threat or not. He took one tentative step towards her. Then another.

Pauline threw Mark at the rat. Her aim was dead-on. The toy soldier hit the exact spot where the rodent had been standing. But the animal's reflexes were quick, and it had disappeared back into its hole by the time the toy had hit the ground.

It took a moment for Pauline to compose herself. When she felt that the danger had passed, she crawled across the floor to retrieve Mark.

"You're a good soldier after all," she whispered, by way of apology. "I'll take good care of you."

Pauline pondered what to do about the hole where the rat had gotten in. She thought of putting her pillow in front of it, but decided that would be unwise. The plump, goose-feather pillow had been a present, given to her by her aunts after Walter died. She didn't want it ruined by sharp, gnawing rat teeth. She was sure she wouldn't be able to sleep without it.

Out of nowhere, the answer came to her. She dragged

the chamber pot from its spot in the far corner and placed it in front of the hole. Then she sat back and grinned, congratulating herself on her ingenuity.

"Those little wheels never stop turning," Mama would have said, tapping Pauline on the forehead. When she was very young, Pauline had believed that the inside of her head actually contained miniature spinning wheels, turning out colorful threads of ideas. She wondered how she ever could have been so naïve.

Her adventure over, Pauline headed back to the mattress. Judging by the sunlight, she guessed it must be close to six o'clock in the morning. Poppa would be getting up to get ready for work any minute now. She needed to sleep, but she was afraid she wouldn't be able to wind down after her experience. Her mind was racing in all directions as she rested her head on the pillow. After a few minutes of tossing and turning, Pauline surprised herself. Not only did she fall fast asleep, but she slept deeper than she ever remembered, without dreams or nightmares. Normally, she was roused by the smallest noise, and slept in nervous spurts. But today, she hibernated. When she finally woke, she was surprised to find Poppa standing over her, looking at her with a curious expression.

"You sick?" he asked.

"No, Poppa," Pauline replied sheepishly. "I must've just been really tired. I'll be right downstairs."

Poppa regarded her with a frown, and she thought he was going to make a disparaging remark, but he turned away and left the room without another word.

It was totally out of character for her to oversleep. She was *always* awake when Poppa came to get her. She prided herself on having a kind of built-in alarm clock, only without the noisy bell. This was the first time it had failed her.

Pauline scurried to get dressed as she listened to Poppa's footsteps, clomping down the stairs. She threw a nervous glance towards the hole where the rat had entered the room. A tiny part of her brain half-expected to see the chamber pot moved away from the wall. Of course, it was still there, right where she'd placed it. She let out a breath of relief.

The sight of it, though, made her realize how badly she needed to use the toilet. She hadn't dared use the pot for hours, given its proximity to the rat hole, so she'd held her water for a long time.

"At least I don't have to clean the thing today," Pauline thought as she hurried down the stairs.

CHAPTER FIVE

"**M**ouse traps?" Poppa asked through a mouthful of bread and gravy. He raised a bushy eyebrow. "I thought you said you saw a rat."

"Yes, Poppa."

Pauline already felt her cheeks burning. She knew what was coming. Poppa had always made a game of making his family feel stupid. They all reacted to this cruel tactic differently. When he did it to Mama, she would get so mad that she'd sass him back. Poppa expected that exact reaction, and would use it as an excuse to hit her. Walter, on the other hand, would be driven to tears by their father's sarcasm. Poppa would then call him a sissy, making Walter cry even harder. A beating invariably ensued. It was rare for Pauline to be the focus of Poppa's wrath. She had always been smart for her age, and possessed the self-restraint that Mama and Walter lacked.

"So..." Poppa continued. "Why would you ask for a *mouse* trap if it's a *rat* you're tryin' to catch? Would you use a rabbit trap to catch a bear?"

"No, Sir." Pauline, embarrassed, avoided looking him in the face.

"Well, then?"

"I didn't know they made traps especially for rats," Pauline tried to explain. Even as she spoke them, she knew her words were inane.

Poppa laughed as if that were the funniest joke he'd ever heard. "I tell you what, Little Girl. I'll give you a piece of cheese to bait it with. All you need is a little crumb, and he'll come to ya. Then I'm gonna give ya a big stick. Would you know what to do with the stick?"

Pauline had only taken a few bites of her dinner. She could feel the small amount of food she'd eaten start to churn in her belly.

"Well?" He drummed his dirty fingers on the table. "Come on. You're a smart girl."

Pauline knew that he wouldn't leave the matter alone until she answered him. "Hit it," she said quietly.

"Hit it how?" he pressed.

"Hit it hard. On the head."

"Why? What if you hit it on the head, Pauline? What would happen?"

"I'd crush its skull."

"That's right, Little Girl. You would crush its skull. Bash its little rat brains in. And you know what else?"

Pauline looked at him, bracing herself for his conclusion. Poppa's eyes were gleaming with pleasure.

"If you have a stick with a sharp end to it, you can use it to…STAB the little critter right through the neck!"

When he said the word "stab," Poppa punctuated it by lifting his fork high in the air and plunging it down with a lightning-quick motion. Pauline moved just in time. The tines of the fork missed her hand by a fraction of an inch, plunging into the roll she'd been holding onto.

Unable to keep her supper down any longer, Pauline covered her mouth with both hands and ran to the bathroom. Even over the sound of her own retching, she could hear Poppa's laughter.

Her gut completely emptied, Pauline took extra time

washing her face and rinsing out her mouth, postponing facing her father as long as she could. She wished she could disappear down the drain like the soapy water. But she knew she had to go back.

When she returned to the table, Poppa had finished his meal. He sat at his place, an empty plate in front of him and a self-satisfied grin on his face. Pauline slid back into her chair and picked up her fork with half a heart. The food on her plate was now cold and unappealing. She poked at it.

"Ain't you gonna eat that?"

"I'm not hungry, Poppa."

"Well, then, give it to me. I'm a starving man!"

Pauline slid her plate over to him and watched him devour its contents. Ignoring the silverware, Poppa used the roll to scoop up the gravy and mashed potatoes, slurping it down with enthusiasm. When he finished, Pauline got up and silently cleared the table.

After she'd done the dishes and swept the floors, Poppa told her to wait while he went outside. When he came back, he held a big tree branch in one hand and his pocket knife in the other. He sat on one of the apple crates and went to work, whistling: "Who's Afraid of the Big Bad Wolf," as he peeled the bark away.

"I just swept!" Pauline thought, watching with disapproval as the wood shavings fell to the floor.

"There you go, girl!" Poppa stood up and handed her the finished project.

Pauline looked it over. Poppa had created a sharp point on one end of the stick. She had to admit to herself he'd done a pretty good job.

"It looks like a real spear, like Joan of Arc had," she remarked, recalling an illustration she'd seen in her history book.

Poppa laughed heartily and patted her on the head. "You just set that aside for now and don't you worry about no rat. Get your thread and needle. You got some mendin' to do. I got holes in my britches!"

CHAPTER SIX

Pauline crawled into bed as the sun was coming up. She put her spear on the floor next to her mattress, where she could quickly grab it if she were awakened by the scritch-scratch of approaching rat feet. As promised, Poppa had given her a small piece of cheddar cheese to bait the rat with. However, after throwing up her dinner, Pauline couldn't ignore her empty, grumbling gut. She ate it herself.

Even though she was exhausted, it took her a long time to fall asleep. As she tried to drift off, she thought about a lot of things. Poppa had actually been *nice* to her tonight, after she'd complimented his work. Prior to that, though, he'd been meaner than usual, teasing her about rat brains. Did he feel bad about making her throw up? Was the spear a kind of "I'm sorry" gift?

Pauline thought of another possibility, although she didn't like it. Maybe if she speared the rat, Poppa would start treating her better. It would be like earning a badge or a medal. He was putting her to the test, she was sure of that much. If she kept passing the challenges he gave her, would he start giving her more and more privileges? Eventually, Poppa might not feel the need to lock her up anymore. And if that happened, would he let her go to school again? The thought both excited and worried her.

My goodness, Pauline thought. *I've already missed so much schoolwork, I might never be able to catch up with the rest of my clas*s.

She figured she'd probably have to repeat the fifth grade. This was a shame, considering she'd always been ahead of most of her class. It would take some getting used to, being with younger kids. She also didn't fancy the idea of re-learning lessons she probably remembered. But compared to being locked in the attic, Pauline decided that getting left back wasn't the worst thing in the world.

One thought melted into another. Pauline felt her eyelids grow heavy with impending sleep, until she sank into the strangeness that was her dream world.

She found herself in their old yard again, wandering around outside the shack where they'd lived for the first six years of her life. Only she was her present age- ten years old- in her dream. What's more, she had a feeling that her family had never left this place.

It was summertime, judging by the vibrant green of the lawn and the surrounding woods. Pauline was playing Hide-and-Seek with Walter. Much to her frustration, she couldn't find him. She could hear him giggling, but his laughter seemed to emanate from under every bush, and behind every tree. Every time she thought she'd found his hiding place, she came up empty-handed. She started to grow cross. She suspected that Walter was hiding near the railroad tracks, the one spot where he wasn't allowed to play.

"Walter! You bad boy! You get away from those railroad tracks!" Pauline hollered as she marched down the slope of their front yard. She could see something- or someone- partially hidden in the brush alongside the tracks. "I'm gonna tell Mama, and she'll tell Poppa! You oughta know better than that!"

"No. *You* ought to know better."

A voice behind her made her jump. She spun around to face Mark. This time, he wasn't life-sized. He was the size of his regular doll self, only a few inches tall. He hopped from branch to branch on a young sapling, until he was eye-level with Pauline.

"What do you mean?" Pauline demanded, as if it were the most ordinary thing in the world to be having a conversation with a living doll.

"I mean, why are you looking for Walter?" Mark asked in an odd, tinny voice. "Walter isn't here. It's your Mama who is here."

Before she could ask him what he meant, Pauline felt the ground start to shake beneath her feet. The train was coming! She grabbed hold of the young tree, and dug her heels into the ground. Her panicked eyes locked with Mark's painted black ones, searching for reassurance. His mouth was a little black "O" of surprise. He lost his balance and went flying off the branch.

"No!" cried Pauline. She turned to see him lying flat on his back on the railroad tracks. Mark writhed and wriggled, like an upside-down beetle, but he couldn't right himself. He looked at her pleadingly, but she was too frightened to move. Meanwhile, the train was thundering closer by the second...

Pauline awoke with a strangled gasp. Her eyes drank in the reality of the familiar room, and she was almost grateful to feel the bumpy mattress beneath her fingertips. Her nightmares were getting progressively stranger, yet they were feeling more and more real. She'd been positive that when she opened her eyes, that she'd be looking up at the bottom of a speeding train.

She reached under her pillow and found Mark. She held him up as close to her face as she could, not knowing what she was looking for. He was a handsome fellow, she supposed. Mama would have described him as "rugged" if he were a real man. He was modeled after a soldier from The Great War. He wore a U.S. Private's uniform, with a helmet and boots. A rifle was slung over his right shoulder. At the most, Mark was only 4 inches tall. His one-dimensional body reminded her of the paper dolls she used to cut out with Ruthie and Mary Rose. His back was painted a solid red. Despite what Poppa had said about Mark being created for the sole purpose of target practice, Walter had told her that this idea was unacceptable.

"I would never, ever shoot a U.S. soldier," he'd vowed, as serious as could be. "I found him, and it's my job to protect him from The Enemy."

Only her brother couldn't even protect himself in the end, Pauline thought sadly.

"What did you mean?" Pauline whispered to the miniature man who'd just played a pivotal role in her dream. "Is Mama alive? Is she hiding out in our old house, Mark?"

She waited, but of course she got no answer from the inanimate soldier. Sighing, Pauline placed him beneath her pillow, and laid back down. She was convinced that her dreams held a hidden message. They'd only started after she found Mark. There had to be a connection. Somebody was trying to tell her something about Mama and Walter.

Or maybe the key was in her own mind. Pauline had *thought* she remembered everything that happened to Mama and Walter, but now she wasn't so sure. As she tried to draw a timeline in her head, and put events in their proper order, she grew less confident that her recollections were accurate. Some of the pictures in her head were fuzzy. Other times, she'd replay a scene in her head, but she could only get so far before it would cut off, part-way through.

The only explanation she could think of was that she had seen something so terrible, she'd willed her memory to erase it. Was it really gone forever? Pauline suddenly felt she couldn't afford *not* to remember.

With dread, she closed her eyes and forced herself to think about the day she was constantly trying to forget.

CHAPTER SEVEN

One blustery night last winter, Poppa had not come home from work at his usual time. Normally, he'd walk through the door no later than 6:30PM (except on Fridays, when he played cards). But, on this particular night, he'd kept his family waiting much longer than usual. Pauline and Walter had exchanged questioning glances, wondering where he could be, but they didn't say anything out loud, because they could see Mama was distressed. It was close to 8 o'clock before she gave up trying to keep dinner warm for him, turning off the stove. She tried to put on a calm face as she cleared his place at the table, but Pauline knew Mama was worried about him. That night's winter storm was far worse than any she'd ever seen. When she peered out the window, the snow looked like a tornado of white confetti. Even though none of them said so, they were all concerned that something bad might have happened to Poppa. Had he been in an accident?

She and Walter were allowed to stay up later than usual that night, and Pauline knew it was because Mama needed their company. When Poppa still hadn't come home by 9:30, Mama sent them off to bed. Pauline hated to leave her Mother all alone to fret, but she did as she was told. She fell asleep wondering if Mama would sit up all night, waiting.

It seemed she had only nodded off for a minute when she and Walter were frightened awake by the slamming of the front door. Their father had finally come home. Although it was the middle of the night, Poppa was loudly cursing at Mama to get his dinner ready. Walter grabbed for Pauline's hand in the dark and she squeezed it.

"Bill! It's 2AM!" They heard Mama object. The voices were coming from the master bedroom. Mama had gone to sleep after all.

Pauline heard a thud, like a heavy object being dropped on the floor. When she heard Mama cry out in pain, she realized that Poppa had dragged her out of bed.

"You do what I say, woman!" Poppa shouted.

A slap could be heard through the thin wall that separated their rooms. Mama made a whimpering noise and Walter began to cry.

"*Shh!*" Pauline pulled her hand out of Walter's and placed it over his mouth. "Don't start. He's gonna come in here next."

Sure enough, Poppa was standing in their doorway less than a minute later.

"You kids get your tails out of bed," he ordered. "Your Ma needs help."

The children rushed to obey him, dressing in the dark in record time. Bleary-eyed and messy-haired, they ventured into the kitchen. Mama stood by the stove, still crying. She held a handkerchief to her face. At first, Pauline thought she was wiping away her tears. Her eyes widened when she saw that the white cloth was spotted with blood. With her free hand, Mama slowly stirred the pot of leftover soup. She didn't seem to notice the children watching her.

"What can I do to help, Mama?" Pauline asked gently, afraid of startling her.

Mama regarded her with an odd look. She seemed

confused by the simple question. Pauline felt a twinge of panic in her tummy. Had Poppa knocked her senseless? But Mama blinked a couple of times, gave her head a little shake, and she composed herself.

"Set the table, please," she said, managing an unconvincing smile. She dabbed at her bloody nose with the handkerchief. "Just your father's place."

Reluctantly, Pauline went through the motions of preparing Poppa's place at the table. It took an extra amount of concentration to perform the task she'd done hundreds of times. Her hands were shaking as she set down a chipped bowl and a rusty soup spoon. All the while, she was praying she wouldn't drop anything.

What Pauline really wanted to do was run back to Mama and hug her. How badly was she hurt? It sounded like she'd landed hard when Poppa jerked her out of bed. What if she had a broken bone and was hiding her pain for her children's sake?

At the same time, Pauline was worried about Walter's welfare. She felt a need to keep an eye on her little brother. With Poppa in the enraged state he was, there was no telling what he might do to the boy.

"Walter!" Poppa's voice boomed from the living room. Pauline heard her brother's light footsteps pad across the floor.

"Yes, Sir?"

"I'm about half-froze to death," she heard Poppa say. "Car stalled 'bout a mile up the road and I had to walk the rest of the ways. Can't be more 'n three or four degrees out there, and snowin' like Hell. Got lost comin' back, 'cause I couldn't see my hand in front of my face for all the damn snow. I need to get warm. Go out and fetch me some wood. This here fire's dyin'. Let's get 'er roarin' up good again."

"Yes, Sir," Walter said in a tired voice. "I'll go put my

boots on."

"You'd better wear your coat and hat, too, young man!" Mama ordered from her post at the kitchen stove. "And don't forget your mittens! They're in your coat pockets."

Flopping into his favorite chair, Poppa mocked Mama.

"Don't forget your mittens," he echoed in a high-pitched voice. "Nag, nag, nag! That's all women know how to do. Ain't my soup hot yet?"

He grumbled to himself a bit more before his voice trailed off. When Pauline glanced his way, he was drinking whisky straight from the bottle.

Walter reappeared, bundled up for his mission, and he headed out into the night. A icy wind blew in before he could shut the door, and Pauline felt the extreme chill go right through her. Poppa must have been mistaken about the temperature. It couldn't be above zero.

Mama had turned off the stove and Pauline was about to summon Poppa to the table when...

Bam-bam-BAM!

Both Pauline and Mama jumped at the sudden, loud noise.

Mother and daughter ran into the living room as Poppa was opening the door. Walter stood at the threshold, his face mostly covered by his hat and scarf. He held his mittened fists in mid-air, ready to knock again. Upon seeing Poppa, he hugged himself and cowered, shivering as snow blew in.

"What the Hell are you doing, bangin' on the door like that?" Poppa yelled. "Where's my firewood?"

"I need a l-lantern, S-sir," Walter said. He was nervous and cold. The combination was making him stutter. "I c-can't see what I'm d-doing."

"Jesus Christ!" Poppa kicked the door so hard that it rattled on its hinges. Walter took a step back.

"What are you, Mongoloid? The woodpile's right around the corner. Can't you find your way around the corner of your own damn house in the dark? Don't you have no sense of direction?"

Walter's eyes flashed with defiance when Poppa challenged his intellect. The little flicker was so brief that Pauline was certain she was the only one who caught it. Her brother had almost sassed Poppa back, but he'd bitten his tongue and tamped whatever retort he had in mind. Before Poppa could assault him with any more verbal jabs, Walter turned around and stomped off, lantern-less, into the night.

"Damn fool boy!" Poppa seethed.

Walter hadn't closed the door behind him. Poppa tried slam it shut, but with the wind working against him, it took an extra bit of effort to close it. Afterwards, he leaned against the door, breathing heavily. Snowflakes were melting in his beard. More snow was turning to puddles around his feet. When he realized that Mama and Pauline were staring at him, Poppa got angry again.

"What are you dames doin', modeling for statues?" he snapped. "Make yourselves useful. Where's my dinner?"

The two of them rushed into action. Mama ladled the soup into his bowl while Pauline buttered his roll. They'd just finished their respective tasks when they heard Poppa throw the bolt on the door.

"Bill, what are you doing?" Mama said, her already-pale face turning ashen.

"Boy needs to learn a lesson," Poppa said, striding over to the table. He sat down and noisily began to slurp his soup.

Mama and Pauline exchanged anxious looks, but neither dared challenge him.

Seconds later, the pounding began. It started out as an

insistent "hurry-up-I'm-cold" knock. The door handle rattled. There was a long pause as it dawned on Walter that it was locked. Then, all at once, the door was subjected to a desperate, double-fisted bashing.

This was the first time Pauline had what she'd come to call one of her "away moments." She didn't know how it was possible, but suddenly, in her mind's eye, she could *see* Walter, locked outside. As if she were a snowbird with a treetop view, Pauline watched her brother grope his way to the snow-covered woodpile and gather a bundle of firewood under one arm. She observed him blindly feeling his way around the corner of the house with his free hand, traipsing through the snow until he reached the front door. She felt helpless as she watched him yank at its handle, eager to get inside and warm up. When he was unsuccessful, he pulled harder, thinking the door was simply stuck. Then, as the truth hit him, he dropped the wood. It vanished, swallowed up by the powdery snow that came up to Walter's waist. Terrified, he started banging away with both hands.

Pauline knew this right away that this scene wasn't just a product of her vivid imagination. She *knew* she was still sitting at the table, but part of her was outside with her brother. She wanted to look away, but something compelled her to watch the awful scene.

"Hey! Hey!" Walter cried in a shrill voice as he knocked.

His voice brought Pauline back to herself. She gripped the edge of the table as if to anchor herself, afraid she might "float away" again.

"Hay is for horses!" Poppa barked, and continued eating.

"Let me in! Please! I'm cold!"

Mama started to rush to the door, but Poppa grabbed

her by the wrist and twisted her arm until she was kneeling on the floor, grimacing in pain.

"Leave 'im be," Poppa said in a warning monotone.

Pauline observed, with grim fascination, that while Poppa gripped Mama's arm with his left hand, he still managed to keep eating soup with his right. He never even splashed a drop on his shirt.

"But Bill! His lungs! He'll get sick!" Mama protested.

"He'll be fine!" Poppa yelled. "Which is something you *won't* be, if you don't let me finish my dinner in peace."

He shoved her to the ground, where she stayed for a minute, covering her eyes and muttering something that sounded like a prayer under her breath. She took a deep breath and dried her eyes with her apron. Pauline helped her to her feet and they stood close together, waiting for Poppa to finish eating.

Meanwhile, the pounding at the door had ceased. Pauline's ears were pricked, listening for a clue as to his whereabouts. Had he tired himself out? Was he leaning against the door, waiting for Poppa to let him in?

No sooner had that thought crossed her mind, when she saw Walter's face pop up in the living room window. Mama gasped. In the short time he'd been outside, he'd lost his hat to the wind. His scarf had come mostly unwrapped from his skinny neck, and it flapped around his head like a red flag in the wind. His blonde hair was wet with snow, plastering it to his head. Walter's oversized mittens made desperate, muffled *thump-a-thumps* on the glass.

"You break that window, I'll break your head, boy!" Papa hollered. He didn't even look up from his bowl.

It was doubtful Walter could hear him over the howling wind, but regardless, he darted out of sight. Seconds later, he was at the kitchen window. His face was red, nostrils flaring. His breath came out in icy clouds. Walter had lost his scarf in the few feet he'd traveled. The relentless storm seemed to be taking a toll on his strength. Instead of knocking, he just pawed at the glass now, scraping the snow off the pane as rapidly as it fell.

Pauline raised a trembling hand to her lips to stifle a scream.

"Bill, *please*. He's suffering," Mama raised her voice. She was staring at her hands, nervously flexing her fingers, as she spoke. Pauline sensed that she was too disgusted with Poppa to look at him, nor could she stand to see her son in such anguish.

"It'll make the boy stronger," Poppa insisted. "Little sissy's got to build up his endurance."

He finished his soup, lifting the bowl to his lips to drink the last drop. He wiped his mouth on his sleeve and looked at Mama.

"Any more?" he inquired.

"No," Mama whispered.

"Hmph." Poppa patted his not-quite full stomach with dissatisfaction.

He rose and stretched. Mama and Pauline stared in silence as he passed them. The food and the whiskey seemed to have taken some of the edge off Poppa's dark mood. His posture was more relaxed as he headed towards the front door. He was less than two feet away from it when he abruptly stopped in his tracks. He made a sharp right turn, to use the bathroom instead. Mama and Pauline fidgeted, nervously waiting for him to finish his business. Both of them kept their eyes glued to the front door, but neither moved a step toward it.

They heard the toilet flush. Poppa emerged and walked to his easy chair.

Oh no, Pauline thought. *He's going to sit down and listen to the radio! He's not going to let Walter back in!*

But Poppa didn't sit. He reached for his bottle of whiskey and took another pull from it.

Satiated, he headed to the front door. His gait was as casual as if he were stepping outside to catch a breath of fresh air on a sunny morning.

Instead of opening the door right away, Poppa paused with his hand on the bolt. He stood with his head cocked, listening. All three of them held their breath. Other than the wind and the distant snap of a branch breaking beneath the weight of heavy snow, there was only ominous silence.

Poppa's bravado dissipated. He looked uneasy now. Picking up on his tension, Mama and Pauline hung a safe distance back, not knowing what to expect. Slowly, he lifted the bolt and gave the door a sharp tug. It swung open, letting in the coldest burst of air Pauline had ever felt.

Snow had piled against the door, and it tumbled inside like a miniature avalanche. It was followed by Walter. He staggered indoors, weaving like a little drunk. He took a few crooked steps, then pitched forward, unconscious.

Mama gasped, and sprang into action. She ran past Poppa as though he didn't exist, and scooped Walter up in her arms. Cooing baby talk to him, she carried him to the fireplace. She knelt before it, cradling her son, even though the fire was barely an ember. Pauline immediately went to work, trying to stoke the fire. She managed to conjure up an anemic flame. She knew it would be useless in warming her brother.

"Is he…" Pauline was afraid to say the "D" word.

"No," Mama cut her off. "He's alive. He'll be fine. Walter! Walter, open your eyes for Mama! Walter!"

She gently patted his reddened cheeks until he blinked and groggily rolled his head from side to side. Mama let her breath out in a little puff of relief. Then she turned to Poppa, looking up at him with an expression of disdain which Pauline had never seen on her mother's face. Normally, Poppa reacted with violence if he thought Mama was being indignant. This time, something in her eyes made him back off.

"Guess I'll have to get my firewood myself," he mumbled, grabbing his coat and heading out the door.

For a second, Pauline thought that Mama was going to throw the bolt on the door, giving Poppa a taste of his own medicine. But if the thought had crossed her mind, it was just as quickly brushed aside. Walter was crying softly now. He needed her undivided attention.

Lovingly, Mama stroked his wet hair. Walter responded by burying his face in her bosom. Pauline was reminded of the baby he'd once been, an infant who was always sick and could rarely be comforted. Neither Mama's lullabies or Pauline's foot-tickling had been able to quiet his sobs. She backed away from Mama and Walter, having no clue how she might be of assistance.

By the time her father came back with a load of firewood, Pauline felt as though she was in another world. She was watching two different picture shows on a movie screen that was split down the middle. In one scene, Poppa was placing logs on the fire, cursing the wood that refused to ignite, and the matches that burned down too quickly, singeing his fingers. On the other side, Pauline watched Mama pick up Walter, as though he were as light as the clothes he had on, and carry him out of the room.

There was a brief intermission, during which the screen went blank. Then Act Two began. On the left side of the screen, Poppa finally got the fire going. On the right, Mama returned with Walter, who was now clad in his striped pajamas. The two sides merged into one scene. Mama took Poppa's place beside the fire, holding Walter next to the warmth of its flames. Poppa rose without a word and retired to his chair. He didn't drink, nor did he turn on the radio. Instead, he sat in silence, staring out the window at the swirling snow. Pauline closed her eyes, letting the scene fade to black.

CHAPTER EIGHT

The weeks that followed dragged on like one continuous, dark day. Walter grew far sicker than he'd ever been. Some good Samaritans from their church came to the house and gave Pauline a mattress to sleep on, so she wouldn't catch Walter's cold. She was allowed to choose one of the empty upstairs bedrooms for her own. After years of wishing for her own bed and her own space, she had both; only now she wanted things back the way they were. She would have traded her privacy for Walter's health in a heartbeat.

Even though Mama and Poppa didn't know how they'd be able to afford it, Dr. Cole was summoned from town.

"Pneumonia," he said, confirming Mama's worst fear.

Father Anderson stopped by one evening. Pauline couldn't have been more surprised. She'd never seen the Priest outside of church. She'd always assumed that he lived there and wasn't allowed to leave.

Mama helped him out of his coat, repeatedly thanking him for walking nearly three whole miles in the cold to visit them. She insisted that he stay for dinner. With Walter bedridden, there was an empty chair at the table, and Father Anderson humbly accepted her invitation.

Pauline felt shy at first, eating in front of such an important man, but quickly found that his presence had a calming effect on her. He had a kind face, and his soft voice was soothing. Until the Priest's visit, Pauline hadn't realized how much it hurt to look at the empty chair where her brother should have been sitting every time she sat down for a meal.

Poppa had been polite to their guest, but he seemed uncomfortable. While Mama conversed freely with Father Anderson about Walter, Jesus, and miracles, Poppa was sullen and preoccupied. More than once, Father Anderson had to repeat himself to get Poppa's attention.

"What? Pardon me, Father," Poppa looked up guiltily from his casserole, then turned his eyes downwards, studying his half-empty dinner plate. "I was lost in thought."

"No need to apologize." Father Anderson held up a peaceful hand. "I take no offense. I will repeat my question... again. What prayers have you said for your son?"

Mama and Pauline exchanged an ephemeral glance and waited, with apprehension, for Poppa's response. They knew he only went to church "for show," wanting the community to view him as a respectable man who took care of his family. But he never read the Bible on his own time. And as far as being able to quote the scriptures? Pauline doubted her father could do it.

Poppa leaned back in his chair. For the first time that evening, he looked the Preacher squarely in the eyes. In the tense seconds that followed, the silence was so complete, that Pauline thought she could hear Walter breathing down the hall in the bedroom.

At last, Poppa spoke.

"St. Gerard, who, like the Savior, loved children so tenderly..." he began.

Mama and Father Anderson immediately bowed their

heads and began to recite the words with him.

"...*Listen to us, who are pleading for our sick child.*"

Pauline vaguely remembered hearing this prayer before, but she could not join the adults in saying the words. She was feeling the same sense of unreality she'd experienced on the night Walter had gotten sick. First, came the sensation of floating away from herself, rising up like a balloon until she reached the ceiling. Pauline became a spectator, sitting in a balcony seat inside a theatre. Her parents and Father Anderson were like actors on a stage. She saw *herself* too, still seated in her chair, looking small and frightened as she watched the grownups pray.

With fascination, Pauline realized that she could even see through the walls. She peered into the room where Walter lay in bed, his chest barely moving up and down with each shallow breath. She wanted to go to him, but she found herself anchored in place.

Watching her brother, Pauline felt her heart break. She'd always been a believer in the healing power of prayer, but she had a revelation that night. Her brother would not be saved by any of the words in the Bible, nor by the finest doctors in the world. God had heard their prayers, but He had already made His decision. Although Walter's heart was still beating, she began mourning him right then and there. Oddly enough, while she felt the deepest remorse for her dying brother, Pauline felt almost as much sympathy for the little girl sitting so forlornly at the table, even though she knew it was herself.

Me, she told herself. *Me, but not me.*

With that thought, the other self- the one that floated above- felt the force of gravity tugging at her. She was being pulled rapidly downwards. There might as well have been a 10-pound bag of flour tied to each of her wrists and ankles. She plummeted, in a stomach-turning freefall, until she was one with the girl at the table again.

"We thank God for the great gift of our son and ask Him to restore our child to health if such be His Holy will. This favor, we beg of you through your love for all children and mothers. Amen."

The words brought Pauline back to reality. She blinked her eyes and took in her surroundings. She was sitting at the table again, feeling a little bit dizzy from her speedy descent. Proof, she thought, that she hadn't imagined it. Whatever was happening to her was real. As real as the three pairs of eyes watching her. The adults were all looking at her expectantly.

"Amen," Pauline whispered, her voice shaky.

"Poor kid." Poppa looked off towards the bedroom where Walter lay. "It wasn't his fault he got caught out in the storm. He should've known better, goin' out in weather like that, him being in poor health to begin with. But who knows how these kids' minds work nowadays. Can't remember bein' that age, myself. I guess they ain't born with common sense. It's something we gotta teach 'em. Don't think we didn't try, Father. We did. Walter just never learned."

Pauline looked at Poppa with disbelief. Was he saying that it was Walter's fault he'd been caught outside in the snowstorm? That he'd gone outside in the worst blizzard of the year on his own accord? How could Poppa lie to Father Anderson- a *Preacher-*, without so much as batting an eye? She tried to get her mother's attention, but Mama wouldn't look at her. Her eyes were focused on a knot in the wooden table.

Struggling to find her own voice, Pauline could not. Her objection was stuck in her throat. She couldn't speak up for her brother, or tell Father Anderson the truth about Poppa. She hated herself for failing Walter.

"I would like to spend some time alone with the boy," Father Anderson said.

"As you wish, " Poppa replied.

When Father Anderson left the room, Mama sat down in the living room and buried her nose in the well-worn pages of her Bible. Poppa went to his own chair and lit his pipe. Neither of them were paying attention to her when Pauline tiptoed to the bedroom that she and Walter shared. She stopped inside the doorway, invisible. Father Anderson knelt beside the bed. Walter was awake, his eyes focused on the Preacher. Studying his face in the candlelight, Pauline sadly observed that he was paler than he'd been as recently as this morning. He seemed to be growing weaker, too. He didn't even have the strength to lift his head.

Father Anderson was speaking so softly to the boy, Pauline couldn't make out the words. But Walter wore a sweet, peaceful smile. This made Pauline feel a little better. At least her brother didn't appear to be in pain. Every so often, he'd give a slight nod at the Preacher's words, intent on absorbing their meaning.

Suddenly, Walter shifted his gaze to Pauline. It caught her off-guard and she started, as if she'd been caught doing something wrong. Although she'd been careful not to make a sound, he'd somehow become aware that she was there. His eyes, which had grown so dull and lifeless, all at once regained some of their spark. Perhaps they were just reflecting the flame of the candlestick on the bedside stand. It could have easily been wishful thinking on Pauline's part. Whether it was a trick of the light or real, she was jolted by her brother's intense stare. Lately, he'd been lost in a permanent fog from the medicine that could not make him better. He was in no condition to converse with her, and could barely articulate his needs to Mama. Pauline had questioned whether he even recognized them anymore.

But he knows me now, she thought, her hopes rising every so slightly.

The lucidity in her brother's eyes was unquestionable. Maybe her premonition had been wrong. Maybe Walter would surprise them all and recover, and when the snow melted, they would once again walk to school together, putting all memories of this horrible, long winter behind them.

Walter seemed to react to the happy picture Pauline had conjured in her mind. He smiled. It was a genuine, Walter-sized grin. That same ear-to-ear smile had won him first prize in a "Beautiful Baby" contest when he'd been not-quite-one-year-old. It was still a winning smile, even now that he was sicker than any child should ever be. It came straight from his heart, so pure and incapable of hate, despite all the suffering he'd known.

Not even Poppa. You don't even hate Poppa, do you? Pauline asked him, without saying a word.

Walter blinked twice.

Pauline froze. She had forgotten all about the game they used to play. During those times when they'd been ordered by Poppa to be quiet "or else," they'd invented secret signs and gestures to communicate silently.

Blink once for Yes, twice for No.

CHAPTER NINE

The angels came for Walter on a quiet morning in late January. For the first time in over a week, the temperature climbed above the freezing mark, and there was no new snowfall.

In her temporary bedroom upstairs, Pauline awoke to the sight of a bright red cardinal peeking at her on her window sill. When she sat up, he flew away.

As soon as she set her bare feet on the wooden floor, she sensed that something was different inside the house. It felt colder, and unnaturally quiet. A wave of silence seemed to have washed over the entire household. She snapped her fingers just to make sure she hadn't gone deaf.

Pauline made her way downstairs. No one else was up yet. She stood in the hallway, debating her next move. Upon waking, she'd had a feeling that her brother had taken a turn for the worse. Had she had a nightmare about him? Pauline couldn't remember. She decided not to wake Mama up and frighten her, just because she had a "bad feeling." She could be wrong. Walter might be fine.

Pauline decided to see for herself. She glided noiselessly down the hallway. The door was already open halfway, so that Mama would hear if Walter called out for her. Pauline stopped at the threshold, in the same spot where she'd watched Father Anderson visit with Walter only the night before. A perfect sunbeam shone through the window onto her brother's dormant frame.

He's so small! Pauline thought, shocked at how much he'd wasted away from his illness. She could see the top of his ribcage where his pajama buttons had come undone. His body barely made a bump beneath the blanket.

She stood there for two minutes, at least, watching his little chest for signs of movement. She saw none. Pauline fought against the flood of emotions that threatened to break her. She'd known this was coming… so why did it still hurt so bad? She told herself she couldn't break down now. She had to be strong for Mama's sake. A single tear ran down her cheek as she took one last look at her brother, who lay bathed in the spotlight of a brand new morning.

"Goodbye, Walter" she whispered.

Pauline tiptoed into her parents' room. The alarm clock by their bed told her that she'd gotten up an hour earlier than usual. She made her way to Mama, who was sleeping peacefully, one delicate hand hanging off the side of the mattress. She observed that her mother and father slept on opposite sides of the bed, with their backs turned towards one another, exactly as she and Walter used to.

With her heart growing heavier by the second, Pauline reached out squeezed her mother's hand. She watched Mama's eyes flutter open and adjust to the morning sunshine. When she saw Pauline standing above her, Mama smiled at first. But something in her daughter's expression quickly caused her face to become a mask of alarm. Before she could ask what was wrong, Pauline spoke up.

"Get up, Mama. I think Walter is gone."

The weeks that followed Walter's death were a blur in Pauline's memory. There was just too much pain, confusion and chaos to sort through. It was easier to cram all the recollections into an imaginary shoebox and stash it

A LITTLE COMPANY

away, out of sight. Still, bits and pieces of those dark days stuck out like rusty nails in an old board, snagging her when she least expected it.

The hardest thing for Pauline to get through was Walter's funeral. She could still see the images of countless relatives, friends and strangers, mulling about outside the church. It seemed none of them knew quite what to say to one another. They were all dressed in black, a sharp contrast to the pure, white snow that covered the ground and the trees. Mama, wrapped in a heavy black cape, cried inconsolably into her handkerchief, oblivious to those who tried to comfort her. Poppa stood with his hands shoved into his coat pockets; his posture straight and stiff as a scarecrow, his eyes just as emotionless. Pauline herself stood apart from her parents, not knowing who to turn to. She'd been aware of somebody holding her hand, but she couldn't remember who. Large, lacey snowflakes fell nonstop. Father Anderson read from the Bible, reciting words that the wind blew away.

After a eulogy that seemed like it would never end, everyone started moving. The men shook hands, and many of the ladies exchanged hugs. The cold weather almost certainly sped up this process. Everyone present seemed eager to head for the relative warmth of their automobiles. Pauline watched the men sweeping the snow off their windshields, while their wives and children bundled inside.

A nagging question kept popping up in her mind. The ground was frozen solid. She'd overheard someone say that they wouldn't be able to bury Walter until the spring thaw. Pauline wondered where they would keep his coffin in the meantime. Would he have to wait until he was actually *buried* until he was allowed into Heaven? She wanted to ask Father Anderson these questions and many others, but she felt foolish. Besides, he was very busy, consoling the mourners who'd come to pay their respects to Walter. She watched the scene, her question unanswered, as Poppa started up the car and drove it away.

After the funeral, their house was bustling with relatives, most of whom Pauline couldn't remember meeting before, although they all knew her name. Men with grim expressions shook Poppa's hand, then sat and smoked with him. Pretty young women sniffled into lacy handkerchiefs. Older ladies lavished attention on Pauline, intent on pinching her cheeks and smoothing her hair. Grandmother Rochefort, Mama's widowed mother, was a stoic figure in a black, high-collared dress that reached her ankles. Pauline shied away from her.

She knew it was disrespectful, but after a couple of days, Pauline found herself wishing that all these well-meaning people would just go away. There were too many of them; aunts who wore too much perfume, and cousins whose names she kept mixing up. They cornered her, coddled her, and cooed words that she, still in a state of shock, couldn't make sense of. *"Sorry... your brother... a shame... Heaven..."* Pauline tried to string the words into meaningful sentences in her head, but they all seemed like beads from different necklaces.

There was food, tons of it, brought to them by parishioners and by friends from town. A couple of families even drove all the way from Watertown to give their condolences and drop off homemade goodies. But the bundt cakes, brownies and the oatmeal cookies could not tempt Pauline's appetite. She felt so sad that Walter wasn't there to enjoy it. His eyes would have popped out of his head if he'd seen all the cakes and cookies! For such a skinny little boy, he could pack his belly full of food- especially sweets- when given the opportunity.

In the days following Walter's death, Mama pretty

much ceased to function. Such a great loss was too much for her. She hardly ever left her bedroom. Now and then, someone would escort Mama, in her nightgown, to the bathroom and back to her bed. She looked more like an apparition than a flesh-and-blood person. Pauline wanted to go to her, but the adults advised her to leave her alone for now; she "needed her rest."

It was strange not to see Mama flitting around the kitchen, making magical meals out of next to nothing. Not only did she stop cooking, but it seemed she'd lost all interest in eating as well. she had to be spoon-fed and cajoled into finishing even half a bowl of soup. Mama was normally a blur of motion; sweeping, dusting and polishing until the last speck of dust was history. She'd always taken pride in her meticulously clean house. Now all of that was being done for her, and she didn't appear to notice or care. Pauline worried that Mama might have developed a sickness worse than her brother's; one that was in her mind. Suppose she never got over Walter's death? She had heard of special hospitals just for crazy people. Would they have to send Mama to a place like that?

Thankfully, Pauline's fears weren't realized. Little by little, Mama came back. Father Anderson was able to do more for her well-being than Dr. Cole. With the Priest's counseling, and the assistance of relatives, Mama re-learned to go through the motions of everyday life. Several ladies from church volunteered their time as well, coming on days when the Father couldn't. Some were the mothers of Pauline's school friends, and Ruthie or Mary Rose would accompany them. Even though the children were only allowed to sit and talk quietly, given the circumstances, their visits were a great comfort to Pauline. Seeing her friends gave Pauline hope that in spite of her heartbreak, life just might return to normal someday.

As Mama grew stronger, the relatives dispersed in twos and threes, until only Mama's brother and his expectant wife, and Grandmother Rochefort remained. Inevitably, the day came when the final houseguests departed, with Grandmother riding in the back of the young couple's automobile. After almost a month, the house was their own again.

That first evening with just the three of them there, none of them knew what to do with themselves. Mama warmed up the remains of a tasteless, potato-and-cheese casserole. The three of them sat around the table, eating without comment or looking at one another. The *clink-clink* of their forks on their plates and the *slurrp* of their lips on the milk glasses seemed amplified to Pauline. Against her will, her eyes kept wandering to Walter's empty chair. It was a morbid souvenir of something precious, now gone forever.

Following dinner, Poppa trudged over to his living room chair and turned on the radio. It had been silent since Walter's death, and he paused in front of it, as though his brain had to remind his hand what to do. He turned the knob, and with a "click," the sound of the President's voice emanated from the speakers. Poppa turned the volume up a little louder than normal before he sat down. He lit his pipe, but held it without smoking it for the longest time, as he stared out the window.

Bedtime was a strange ordeal. It was her first night sleeping downstairs again. The relatives had an idea to rearrange the bedroom Pauline and Walter had shared, so it wouldn't remind her so much of the past. Pauline thought this was silly, since there were only four pieces of furniture; the bed, the nightstand, their toybox and a shared dresser. Still, she'd smiled politely and thanked her Aunts and Uncles when they moved things around. When they asked her if she thought the room looked better, she nodded and hoped her affirmative response was convincing. The donated mattress was brought down from upstairs, and placed on the bed frame in her and Walter's old room. The mattress that she'd shared with her brother since he was big enough to sleep outside a crib- the one he had died on- was taken away. Pauline thought she remembered someone saying it would be burned.

It took awhile to get used to sleeping faced in a different direction, but Pauline finally managed to nod off. She didn't have nightmares like she'd expected, but she often woke up on Walter's side of the bed.

CHAPTER TEN

I t was the "new" mattress that she laid upon now, in her bleak attic space. Poppa had dragged it up the stairs when he first confined her to her new quarters. She tossed, turned and twisted, but could not find a comfortable position. She felt lumps that she'd never noticed before, reminding her of the old "Princess and the Pea" fairy tale.

She'd felt a little chilled when she first lay down, and curled up in a ball beneath the musty sheet. But she kicked it off now, feeling too warm. Flat on her back, she stared up at the ceiling. The full moon looked like a polished silver dollar, tucked behind the branches of the century-old oak tree outside her window. Together, they painted a complex labyrinth of shadows on the ceiling above her. Pauline busied herself finding hidden pictures in the tangles and twists; A spider's web, with a bird caught in it. The wind picked up, making it look as though the bird was flapping its wings in a desperate attempt to break free. Pauline changed her position on the bed, so that she could view the shadowy collage upside-down. The images she saw now were strikingly creepier.

Faces. Dozens of them. The more Pauline squinted, the more pronounced their features became. There was a man with heavy-lidded eyes, bushy eyebrows and a wild beard. A woman from the last century, with a long face and pointy chin, her hair done up in a tight bun. A hollow-cheeked little boy with doleful eyes. The one common factor that this eerie population shared was sadness. All of these strangers seemed to be suffering. It made Pauline think of a scary drawing she'd seen in her Sunday School Bible, depicting souls doomed to Hell.

The wind picked up even more, and the motion made the shadow-faces animated. Some looked like they were weeping; others, like they were screaming for mercy. Pauline wanted to scream herself, but the sound froze in her throat. Although she was now very tired, her sleepy eyes remained open, glued to the freak show above her. Eventually, clouds covered the moon and the faces disappeared. Pauline lay still in the darkness, afraid to move. A palpable wave of dread washed over her. Somehow she knew the horror wasn't over yet.

Just as sleep came to beckon her, Pauline felt a hand brush across her face. Her eyes snapped wide open. Nobody was there.

A spider! she thought, shuddering. *Oh, yuck! A spider just crawled across my face!*

But, no. The feeling had been more like a smooth, silk glove, sweeping across her entire face. She was almost positive that it hadn't been a spider or any kind of bug. She knew she wasn't dreaming, and she didn't think she believed in ghosts, but...

Her eyes glanced upwards. The clouds had moved on, allowing the moonlight to shine in once again. The earth had turned just enough so that the patterns on the ceiling had changed. Instead of the small, intricate faces she'd seen before, there were vague figures. Long-limbed dancers swayed in the wind. Pauline watched the strange ballet with drowsy interest.

Suddenly, the hypnotic swaying stopped. The shadows

grew darker, larger. When they resumed their action, their motions were jerky and violent. The arms that had stretched gracefully towards the heavens now thrashed about with malevolence. It looked like two people fighting. Or, to be more accurate, one person beating up on another; a victim much smaller than himself.

Pauline gasped. She was remembering something else.

No. I don't want to remember! She protested in her head.

She closed her eyes tightly, and tried to stop the reels from rolling, but it was no use. The movie kept playing on the backs of her eyelids. Poppa, madder than he'd ever been. Hurting Mama real bad. Not just beating her, but wrapping his strong hands around her neck and squeezing the very breath out of her.

Pauline had been there with them. She could see herself, crouched on the floor beneath the kitchen table. Yes, that was the way that it had happened. She'd seen the whole thing. From her hiding place, Pauline had seen Mama's shoes rise up off the floor. It had taken a few dazed seconds for her to comprehend what was going on. Poppa was holding her by her neck, a few inches off the ground, hanging her.

Why, Poppa, why? Pauline screamed in her head.

She concentrated as hard as she could, knowing there was more that she couldn't remember. It was right there, at the edge of her memory, teasing her with its nearness. She reached for it, felt her fingertips brush its surface. Then, before she could grasp it, the memory leaped out of her reach.

When she looked up again, the shadows looked like what they were; mere silhouettes of the branches of the ancient oak tree. The wind had died down and all was as still as could be. Pauline lay wide awake, watching the sky

turn from coal-black, to the indigo of approaching morning.
Shortly before sunrise, she first heard the sound.

Tap-tap-tap.

The noise was coming from the wall opposite her.
Pauline propped herself up on one elbow and listened. A
few seconds later, she heard it again.

Tap-tap-tap.

It sounded like somebody lightly tapping their
fingernails on a glass or a teacup. The odd noise ceased and
was replaced by a soft, steady, crunching sound.

What on earth? Pauline wondered.

Suddenly, she knew. The sound was coming from the
area where she'd moved the chamber pot. It was blocking
the hole where the rat had gotten in. Now the rat wanted
out. It had tip-tapped its tiny nails against the porcelain pot
in frustration. When that did no good, he got smart. He
was now gnawing at the wall to make the hole bigger,
determined to work his way around this bothersome barrier.

Her body ridden with goosebumps, Pauline rose from
her mattress and picked up the stick Poppa had given her.
Not that she believed she could really bring herself to use
it. She'd never killed anything before, aside from swatting
pesky mosquitoes in the summertime. But that was in self-
defense. The rat wasn't threatening to hurt her in any way;
he was probably just hungry. Or maybe he thought he was
defending his territory. Pauline couldn't really blame him
for that, since he'd probably been a resident of the attic
long before Pauline moved in. She wondered why she was
afraid of something so much smaller than herself.

Using this newfound logic, Pauline moved the chamber
pot away from the wall with trembling hands. She heard a
scuttling sound as the startled rat retreated. She waited,
holding her breath, as she tightened her grip on the stick.
She held it vertically, standing statue-still, and waited to

see what the rodent would do next.

Squeezing out of the hole inch by cautious inch, the creature ventured out into the open. In the semi-light, Pauline could see the thing more clearly, and the sight was enough to make her courage start waning. The rat was bigger than she'd remembered; in fact, larger than any rat she'd ever seen. Its black fur was matted and dirty. Its feet were pink, with long, spindly toes that had sharp little nails at their tips. The rat stopped in its tracks when it noticed Pauline. He retreated a few steps and paused, regarding her with beady eyes.

Their silent face-off lasted a good minute or so. Pauline, fairly confident that the rat was not going to charge at her, lowered the stick to waist level. She watched the rat with curiosity now, rather than revulsion. As if sensing that danger had passed, the animal began to go about its business, exploring the room, sniffing around the floorboards.

"There's no crumbs for you to find," Pauline said. "I'm sorry I ate your cheese."

Not that the rat looked like he was starving. He was quite plump. He'd obviously discovered a place where he could always help himself to a good meal.

The rat ignored her chatter. He was eager to get to work, whatever his mission might be. More intrigued than afraid now, Pauline kneeled to watch the rodent's escapades, setting the stick down in front of her. As he sniffed around the edges of her mattress, Pauline felt guilty for her murderous intentions.

He's just trying to survive, like I am, she thought.

The rat found a hole in the side of the mattress and stuck his snout inside. He pulled out a mouthful of cotton stuffing. Pauline's first reaction was to object, but all at once, the rat was running towards her, and her old fear set in. She froze as he scurried past her and disappeared into his hole. She heard him bustling about inside the wall and figured he was building a nest. She supposed she could spare a little cotton if the rat needed to make itself a comfortable bed. Soon, the animal reappeared, gathered another mouthful of cotton, and transported it back to his home.

Feeling a twinge of compassion, Pauline decided to help. She grabbed a couple handfuls of stuffing from inside the mattress and placed them beside the rat's entryway. When he reappeared and saw the surprise gift, the rat retreated, as if he thought he was about to walk into a trap. Moments later, he cautiously peeked out. Pauline grinned as the rat got brave enough to leave the safety of his hole. He sniffed suspiciously at the pile of cotton. When he decided that it wasn't a trick, he eagerly snatched as much as he could in his mouth, and scooted back into the wall to add it to his nest. It took him three trips to retrieve all the material. When he came out one last time to make sure he hadn't missed anything, the rat faced Pauline and stood up on its hind legs. He stared at her for a few seconds, as if wondering what the heck this human girl was doing in *his* attic, and why was she being so nice to him? He dropped back to all fours and disappeared into the wall.

Pauline sighed, feeing lonely. The sun was slowly rising. It was time for her to go to sleep. Poppa would be getting up soon to get ready for work. She needed her rest, so she'd have the energy to do the required cooking and cleaning when he got home. Realizing she was, in fact, quite sleepy, she used the chamber pot and then crawled into bed, falling almost immediately into a dream.

CHAPTER ELEVEN

Pauline was standing in the yard, at their old house by the railroad tracks. She'd come to expect this now, every time she went to bed. She would have been surprised if she dreamed of being anywhere else.

When they'd lived there, Pauline hated the place. The roof leaked, and there were more places for drafts to get in than could be patched up. Many of the window panes had broken; some by bad weather and others by items thrown by Poppa when he was drunk. They couldn't afford to replace them with new glass, so Poppa had boarded them up with wood he got for free from the lumber mill. This did the job of keeping the rain and the snow out, but as a result, the house was always dark and had a permanent gloominess about it. It was also too small for a family of four.

"Cramped," Mama had called bitterly it. "Even for a small family like ours. You can hardly take a step without bumping into someone."

For Pauline and Walter, it meant that there was nowhere to hide from Poppa when he was on the warpath. They'd all been glad to leave that place behind.

Yet, in her dream, Pauline wanted *in*. She walked around and around the outside of the house, running her hand along its boards. There was something different about it since she'd last seen the house. But what? Her eyes scoured the building for changes. Her heartbeat increased as the truth registered. She thought it must be a mirage. It had to be.

There was no door!

Pauline ran in circles around the house until she was breathless, sure she was mistaken. She expected to find that it had been boarded up, or painted over; cleverly hidden so she wouldn't find it, but she was wrong. There wasn't even a hole in the side of the building where the door *should* have been. She supposed it could have had been ripped off its hinges by Poppa, if he was mad enough. But why wouldn't he have replaced it? It was as if a door had never been there at all. There was no way to get in, unless she climbed through a window.

Why would Poppa take out the door? Pauline wondered, trying not to panic. *He must have done it while I was in school. But how'd he patch the wall up so quickly?*

She circled the house again, but to her dismay, all sides of the house looked exactly the same. She noticed something else; the windows had all been repaired, with clean, new panes of glass.

Baffled, Pauline pressed her face up to one of the windows and peered inside. She gasped.

Mama and Walter sat at the kitchen table. They were laughing and joking together. Walter was eating cookies and had crumbs all over his face. He was talking with his mouth full, but Mama didn't seem to mind. She was busy cutting recipes out of The Ladies' Home Journal, but she'd put her scissors down every so often to wipe Walter's face with a napkin, or to playfully muss his hair. Pauline felt jealous. She rapped on the window, softly at first. When they didn't look up from their conversation, she knocked louder. Still, they didn't acknowledge her.

Angry now, Pauline pounded the window with her fist. She knew that she might break the glass and get in big trouble, but she didn't care. Heck, she *wanted* to break the glass! How dare they ignore her and shut her out like this? Where was Poppa?

"They can't hear you."

Pauline spun around. She knew Mark's voice by now. He stood a few feet away, leaning against a tree. His appearance had changed again. He was the height of a real man, and his body had taken on the form of a cartoon figure. His painted-on eyes looked almost expressive, and his black slash of a mouth moved realistically when he spoke. His face was now capable of conveying emotions. In fact, he looked almost sympathetic.

"They're not ignoring you," Mark said, pulling a cigarette out of his pocket and lighting it with a Zippo. He took a long drag and blew a perfect smoke ring before speaking again.

"You see, your Mama and Walter are in a different place," Mark explained. "You can see them, but they can't see you. They can't hear you, either, no matter how hard you knock on those windows."

"Why not?" Pauline shouted. She knew it was babyish, but she stomped her foot in frustration. There were hot tears streaming down her face now, and she was embarrassed, but she pressed on. "And why isn't there any door? Why can't I go inside?"

Mark looked at her sadly.

"Am I… dead?" she asked him, in between frenzied breaths.

Mark cocked his head and looked at her strangely, much as the rat had done.

"What's 'dead'?" he asked.

Pauline's eyes snapped open. She felt as though she'd

been awakened by an electric shock. All the muscles in her body tensed as she realized that someone was standing over her, watching her. This was not part of her dream. It was Poppa.

Pauline gulped, too scared to move. Was she in trouble? Poppa seemed to be in a trance, his eyes wide and moonstruck. She'd never seen such a queer expression on his face before.

"I overslept, didn't I?" she said, in a voice she hoped sounded calm. "I'm sorry, Poppa."

Poppa looked confused for a moment. He shook his head to clear it, gazed back down at Pauline, and ran a hand nervously through his messy hair.

"Can't sleep your life away," he mumbled, stalking out of the room. Pauline shivered as she listened to his heavy work boots stomping down the attic stairs.

She had to take several deep breaths before she could sit up. She waited until her heart slowed from a rapid gallop to a steady trot. As she reached for her shoes, Pauline realized she was holding something in her hand. She looked, and was surprised to see she'd been clutching Mark without even realizing it. She must have pulled him out from under her pillow in her sleep. The tin soldier felt warm against her skin. All at once, she realized that he was growing increasingly hot! Alarmed, Pauline tossed the doll onto her pillow and examined her hand. There was a pinkish-red outline of the doll, like a burn mark, in her palm. In mere seconds, it vanished.

"Pauline!" Poppa's voice boomed from downstairs.

"Coming, Poppa!" she called, scrambling into her shoes. She cast a nervous glance at Mark, but he'd gone back to being just a regular doll. She shook off a chill.

Minutes later, as she stirred the pot of split pea soup, she replayed the incident in her mind. Pauline was certain that the burn mark on her hand hadn't been imaginary. It would be easy to write it off as a leftover fragment of her weird dream. The strange little soldier doll that her brother had left behind was more than a painted man of tin. It wasn't just a link to her past, either. She had a strong feeling that it held a connection to her to her future as well. She needed more pieces of the puzzle to figure it out, but she was determined to solve the mystery.

Poppa drank even more than usual that night. He reclined in his chair, his head lolling to one side. He looked asleep, if not passed out altogether. Pauline looked from him to the door; back and forth, as minutes ticked away. Was he *really* sleeping, or just resting his eyes? Was he testing her loyalty, to see if she'd try to run away? She had to admit now, that she didn't know Poppa as well as she thought she did. For all she knew, maybe he *wanted* her to try and run away, just so he'd have an excuse to do to her what he'd done to Mama. Maybe she was becoming more of a burden than anything else.

Poppa began to snore softly. Pauline tried to summon up her courage. Did she dare sneak out the door? She knew that Poppa had recently oiled the hinges, so that there would be no give-away squeak if she summed up the nerve to oh-so-carefully open the door and slip out into the night. The temptation was *so* great, but... if Poppa were to wake up after she'd set out down the long, dirt road to town, he'd have no trouble catching up to her in the Ford. If she tried to hide in the woods, he'd just hunt her down. Once he got a hold of her, she wouldn't have to worry about being confined to the attic anymore. Pauline had come to the conclusion that Poppa was incapable of feeling either love or remorse. She couldn't decide which was worse.

There! There it was again; a flash of a memory, as quick and slippery as an eel. She'd just started to touch on that elusive *something*, when Poppa stirred. He looked at her with bloodshot eyes, then struggled to make out the hour on his watch.

"Half past midnight," he slurred. "You'd better get yourself upstairs."

Pauline nodded and turned to go.

"I'll be up in a minute to tuck you in."

Pauline spun around to face him with such an astounded look, Poppa burst out laughing. He'd meant the words as a joke, and her shocked reaction tickled him. Pauline felt her cheeks burning as she retreated, her father's laughter still ringing in the background.

CHAPTER TWELVE

When Pauline awoke the next morning, she could tell by looking at the bright sun that it must be getting close to noon. She'd slept later than usual. That was a good thing, because it meant fewer hours of boredom, waiting for Poppa to get home. She felt refreshed by her dreamless sleep. She hadn't realized until now, how exhausted she was after having one of her dreams about Walter and Mama.

And Mark, she reminded herself.

Gingerly, she plucked the doll out from under her pillow, leery of getting "burned" again, but he was cool to the touch. She examined him close-up. He looked the same as ever, with hardly any chips in his paint, only the familiar dent in his midriff. She held him as tight as she could for a whole minute, to see if he'd heat up again, but his temperature remained normal.

Pauline wondered if Mark missed Walter. She quickly berated herself for thinking something so crazy. Dolls couldn't think or feel! Was she losing her mind? It would be understandable, given all she'd been through, but she wouldn't let herself go crazy. She needed to stay sharp if she was going to devise a plan to get away from Poppa. Yet, there was no denying that Mark had become very important to her. He was her only tangible connection to her late brother, and Pauline had also come to think of him as a sort of good luck charm. After all, wasn't he always trying to help her in her dreams?

"I wish I were smarter," Pauline said, lying on her back. She held Mark upright on her chest and spoke to him directly. "I *used* to be smart. I got all A's in school. So shouldn't I be able to figure a way out of this mess? I think it's that I've been kept out of school for so long; that's the problem. I'm losing my smart-ness. Is that possible? I can't say anything to Poppa. I know he won't let me go back. And he can't teach me himself." Here, she lowered her voice, even though no one was around to overhear the secret she was about to tell.

"Did you know Poppa only went to school up until sixth grade?" she whispered. "I'm only in fifth, but I can read and write better than he can. Of course, I'd never actually say that to him. He'd kill me!"

Her own words chilled her. She hadn't meant the phrase literally, but she still wished she hadn't said it. The truth was the truth, however. Poppa was a killer. She couldn't take tomorrow, or even her next breath, for granted.

Although she tried to avoid thinking about it, there was a question always lurking in the back of her mind: What were Poppa's plans for her? Certainly, he couldn't expect to keep her locked in a room, released for only a few hours a day to cook and clean, for the rest of her life? When would he let her go?

The way he'd been looking at her when she woke up yesterday unnerved her. She got a chill, even now, remembering. How long had he been standing there, watching her while she slept? A minute? An hour? The possibility made her skin crawl.

Poppa's recent comment about how much she looked like her mother didn't rest well with her, either. If she was starting to remind him of Mama, was she in danger? What if Poppa got so drunk that he got the past confused with the present and completely mistook Pauline for his late wife? He might even call her "Mary" by accident. She had no idea *what* she'd do if this scenario came true. Pauline wished she could remember what Mama had done or said to make Poppa so angry on the night she died. At all costs, she must avoid doing the same thing, if she wished to stay alive.

"Dear God," she prayed aloud. "Please, help me remember. I've tried and tried, but I need Your help. Oh... and if Mama and Walter are with You, send me a sign. Will You do that for me, God? I've been good. Will You tell them I love them and that I miss them very much? And please watch over me and keep me safe. Don't let Poppa hurt me. Thank You. Amen."

The rest of that day held a couple of surprises for Pauline. Poppa had shot a rabbit, so they had something besides vegetables in their stew for a change. Pauline made Poor Man's Bread to go along with it, and their bellies were as full as could be by the time the last crumb was gone.

"I tell you what!" Poppa slapped the table so hard that the silverware jumped. "If you keep cookin' meals like that, I'll be shootin' rabbits, woodchucks, deer... pretty much anything on four legs to bring home to ya! You're a better cook than your mother ever was. You'll make a fat man outta me yet!"

Pauline gave him a half-smile, knowing that this was Poppa's version of a compliment, but hearing him mention Mama made her feel sad.

Poppa's expression grew serious. At first she thought he was upset that she'd smiled, but he changed the topic altogether.

"This house, Pauline," he said somberly. "Do you like

this house at all?"

Pauline didn't know how she was expected to respond.

"I don't." he continued, without waiting for an answer. "In fact, I've been thinkin' lately that I hate this big, ol' place. This house holds a lot of bad memories."

Pauline nodded. He wasn't going to get any argument from her there.

"What do you say we move?" Poppa suggested.

"But... Where would we go?" Pauline asked, shocked. "What about your job?"

"My Uncle Cal... You only met him once, when you was a baby. He'd be my Pop's youngest brother. Lives up in Minnesota. Been out of touch for quite a few years. Well, what with all that's gone on lately, you know... Walt dyin' and your Ma runnin' off..."

Pauline blinked in surprise, but caught herself before she reacted any further. No matter, because Poppa wasn't even looking at her as he spoke. He was staring off into space.

"I thought it'd be best to write him a letter," Poppa continued. "Took me awhile. You know me an' writin'."

Pauline was watching him closely, analyzing his face for a clue as to what might be going on in his mind. He wasn't drunk, and he didn't appear to be lying. The only conclusion she could draw was that Poppa had come to believe the story he'd concocted to cover his murderous tracks. He had convinced himself that Mama had run off with another man. He didn't remember killing her!

"So I finally heard back from Uncle Cal 'bout a week ago," Poppa went on. "He's been workin' at the same logging company for goin' on forty years now. Been the boss of it for the last twenty. Said he'd be happy to give me a job there, and we're welcome to stay in his house if we earn our keep. His wife's had a stroke and needs nursin'. I told him I think you'd be pretty good at helpin' her out. Some extra bodies and pairs o' hands would make a big difference for them."

Pauline contemplated this. Minnesota was a long ways from New York. She'd only been out-of-state once, when she was eight years old. They'd driven to Connecticut to visit Mama's brother and his family for Thanksgiving. The ride had seemed to take forever. Driving all the way to Minnesota would feel like at least three forevers, especially if she were all alone with Poppa.

But he was right about the house holding too many memories. Every time she turned around, she expected to see Mama taking a piping hot loaf of bread from the oven, or Walter in his striped pajamas, drawing pictures of ships and airplanes with their Crayolas. Maybe if they moved away, her nightmares would stop.

Or, it might be my chance to escape, she thought. Somewhere between here and Minnesota, she could make her getaway. Poppa would have to stop for gas and to eat. She would have many chances to make a run for it. All she needed to do was to summon up enough courage.

"When would we leave?" she asked.

"Soon as possible. 'Course we gotta sell the house first. She should bring in a pretty penny. We'll have *money*, Little Girl." Poppa's eyes twinkled at the thought. "Do you remember us ever havin' money?"

Pauline shook her head "no." Poppa laughed at her serious expression.

"Things are gonna change, Little Girl," he declared. "Things are changing already."

CHAPTER THIRTEEN

The sky was blacker that night than she'd ever seen it. It looked to Pauline as though God had spilled a bottle of ink on the canvas of the sky, obscuring the moon and the stars. Poppa'd mentioned that he'd seen thunderheads rolling in on his way home from work, and that there could be an ugly storm coming. She believed his prediction.

Poppa held a lantern above their heads as he followed her up the stairs, but its beam barely penetrated the darkness. Pauline could only see a foot or so ahead of herself. The black abyss before them seemed to drink up the light. She'd never been afraid of the dark, but combined with the approaching storm and the changes in Poppa, it was enough to spook her tonight.

She laid down on her mattress as usual, but as Poppa started to close the door and lock it, Pauline called out to him.

Poppa's face appeared, bathed in yellow-orange lamplight. Pauline couldn't tell if his expression was one of impatience or curiosity.

"It's too dark," she said in a small voice. "There's no moon."

"What do you want me to do?" he asked, a hint of mockery in his voice. "You think I can wave a magic wand

and make the moon shine or the sun rise?"

Pauline felt the muscles in her neck and shoulders tense. It had been a good day so far, and she wasn't about to let Poppa ruin it by making her feel stupid. She bit her lip to make sure there would be no hint of sass in her voice before she spoke again.

"Please, Poppa... Can you bring me up a candle?" she implored in the sweetest voice she could muster. "I'd feel a whole lot better."

"What's it matter? You're going to sleep," Poppa said. "Your eyes'll be closed. It'll be dark anyways."

Pauline couldn't think of a comeback. Her father's words were perfectly logical. At a loss, she just repeated: *"Please?"*

Poppa stared at her for a minute, then disappeared without saying a word. Pauline lay still, listening to the familiar sound of his footsteps descending the creaky staircase. There was complete silence for so long that Pauline thought that he'd either forgotten her request or had decided not to fulfill it. But after a few minutes passed, she heard him climbing back up.

"Will this do, Queenie?" Poppa had the lantern in one hand and what remained of a white taper candle in the other. Its little flame fought mightily against the oppressive darkness.

"Yes, Poppa," Pauline said, genuinely grateful. "Thank you."

Poppa placed the candle, in its rusty holder on the floor, a safe distance from the mattress. As he straightened up, his eyes never left Pauline. Invisible, icy fingers grazed her back and gave her gooseflesh. She couldn't decipher the strange looks that he'd been giving her lately. Sometimes it seemed he was looking right through her, and other times she felt like he was peering *into* her; dissecting her thoughts and analyzing her motives.

The metallic "click" of the key turning in the lock was a welcome sound. Poppa was gone, without a "good night" uttered by either of them. Pauline rolled onto her side and focused on the flame, letting it hypnotize her. She felt soothed, and sleep began to entice her.

The storm broke all at once, jolting Pauline awake. She sat up in a panic. It sounded as though a dozen cannons had been fired, in a rapid row. She wrapped her arms around her legs and hugged herself this way until she stopped shivering. Pulling the sheet up to just above her nose, Pauline peeked, wide-eyed, at the commotion outside her window. The sky lit up with terrific flashes of lightning, so close together that it seemed like a never-ending chain of explosions. Big bangs accompanied this light show, sounding like giant barrels of exploding gunpowder. The rain came down in angry, little drops that were so close together, they seemed to form a solid sheet of water. They pelted the window pane, like a thousand tiny fists. The powerful wind wrestled with the old oak tree. The way its branches thrashed so wildly about, it resembled an angry octopus caught in a net.

Almost unconsciously, Pauline reached beneath her pillow for Mark. Her hand felt around, but found nothing. She frowned. The storm no longer the focus of her attention, she searched the mattress and the tangled bed sheet for the doll. No Mark. Next, she groped along the mattress's sides, thinking he must have fallen onto the floor. She searched the perimeter around the bed once, twice, three times, but she came up with nothing but fingers full of dust.

Refusing to believe Mark was gone, Pauline grabbed the candle and conducted a room-wide search. The thunderstorm was merely background noise, as she crawled along the floor, looking for her soldier friend. Thoughts that would never have crossed her logical brain a few months ago, ran amok now: Had Walter somehow come back to reclaim his favorite toy? Could the rat have stolen it? Had Poppa come in and slipped it out from beneath her pillow without waking her? Nothing was impossible in her crazy new world.

When it finally hit her that she wasn't going to find the doll, Pauline sat in the middle of the floor and broke into tears. She didn't try to stop them. She let them fall freely, the noise of the thunder and rain covering up her sobs.

"Oh, I hate you, I hate you, I HATE you for leaving me!" she blubbered to Mark, wherever he might be. "How could you leave me all alone again?"

By the time her sobs had diminished and she'd exhausted her body, the storm was still going strong outside. Pauline was no longer spooked by it. She had calmed down enough to want to return to bed. Sleep seemed like a lovely idea.

Just when she'd crawled onto the mattress, a bolt of lightning hit the oak tree. Gaping at the scene outside her window, Pauline let out a little scream as the regal oak split in half with a deafening crack. Half of it remained standing; the other half fell in a slow-motion bow of defeat.

Once she'd gotten over her shock, Pauline mourned the loss of the tree. It was hard to believe something so ancient and strong could be destroyed in a split second. Observing the violent storm, which was showing no signs of weakening, she wondered if perhaps the end of the world had begun. She'd never seen God so furious.

Something soft brushed against her hand. She grabbed the candle to see what it was. It was the rat. Normally, she would have cringed with revulsion at having been touched by a filthy rodent. But tonight she just didn't care. Nothing could scare her anymore. Pauline found his behavior curious. Since when was he tame enough to approach her so boldly? Had he been some little boy's pet at one time? Was he just so scared by the storm that he didn't know what he was doing?

Something else caught her attention. She looked closer, wondering if her eyes were playing tricks on her. Another flash of lightning revealed that, no, she wasn't seeing things. The rat was dragging something in its mouth.

Pauline leaned towards the rat to get a closer look. To her surprise, it didn't back away. The normally skittish animal no longer seemed fearful of her. It stood still, as tame as any domesticated cat, as she hunkered down, almost nose-to-nose with it,.

"What have you got there, little one?" she whispered, moving her hand slowly, so she wouldn't frighten the creature.

Ready to draw her hand back quickly, in case it tried to bite her, Pauline got her fingers close enough to touch the long strip of whatever-it-was that the rodent held in his mouth. She pulled at it, expecting a struggle, but the rat readily relinquished its hold. Not only that, but he remained where he was and watched her, as if waiting to see her reaction.

Baffled by the rat's odd mannerisms, but more interested to see what she'd confiscated from it, Pauline fingered the item, trying to guess what she held. Just a piece of an old rag? No, something smooth. A ribbon! It had to be. She held it up to the candlelight and saw she was right.

"Did you bring me a present?" Pauline teased, smiling at the rat. It regarded her for a second or two longer, then turned tail and scampered back into its hole.

She guessed that the ribbon had been part of the rat's

nest at one time. Was this his way of thanking her for giving him the bedding?

Another spectacular flash of lightning gave her a better look at her "gift." The ribbon was dark blue. It didn't seem to be very old; it wasn't brittle, or even very dirty. She wondered where the rat could have gotten it. The more she stared at it, the more it looked almost... familiar.

CHAPTER FOURTEEN

A sensation, almost like motion sickness, hit her hard. Pauline felt like she was riding backwards on a runaway train. She flailed her arms to steady herself, forgetting she was already kneeling on the floor. Her head reeled as she was jerked back in time. A time not so very long ago… it only *seemed* that way.

It was a sunny afternoon. She was in her parents' bedroom, standing with Mama in front of the mirror that hung over the dresser.

"See? It matches your dress." Mama was smiling at her. She'd just surprised her daughter with a new hair ribbon.

Pauline was wearing one of the two dresses she owned. There was her pretty Sunday dress; pale yellow, with a full skirt and lacey bodice. Mama had splurged, in spite of Poppa's claim that it was a "waste of money," and ordered it for her from a Montgomery Ward catalogue. It was the prettiest dress she'd ever seen, and she would have liked to have worn it every day. However, it hung in her bedroom closet six days of the week.

Her "everyday" dress was the one she had to wear the rest of the time. She hated it. She'd always thought it was ugly, but Pauline never complained, because she didn't want to hurt Mama's feelings. She'd worn it for a good year, and the dress was now threadbare and too small for her. Even though Mama had let the hem out all the way, it still rode an inch above her knees. It had once been navy blue, but it had faded to a dark, grayish shade, more like the color of clouds reflected in a rain puddle. She disagreed with her mother about the pretty ribbon matching her dress, but she didn't say so.

Mama had been to town earlier that day with her friend, Betsy Butterfield. Poppa had given her money to buy him some shoe polish and new suspenders. Mama had been brave enough to ask her husband to give her an extra bit of cash to buy Pauline some much-needed new underthings, and "odds and ends" for herself. When Poppa complied without any argument, Pauline was astonished. She wondered if he was feeling guilty about Walter, and trying to make it up to Mama.

Betsy's green Chevrolet had just pulled up in front of the house as Pauline was walking home from school. Pauline's eyes widened when she saw all the bags and boxes in the back seat.

"Why Pauline!" Betsy chirped, sticking her head out the car window. "You're getting so big! Look how tall you are! And pretty, too! Why, it won't be long before the young fellows will be fighting over which of them will get to carry your schoolbooks home for you!"

Pauline blushed and giggled, then eagerly helped Mama carry her purchases into the house. Only about a quarter of the packages in the car were hers; Betsy had done the majority of the shopping. Still, her Mother had come home with much more than what had been on her original shopping list. Pauline hoped that Poppa wouldn't be too mad.

Indeed, besides the two items Poppa had specifically requested, Mama had bought new socks and underwear for all three of them, the blue hair ribbon for Pauline, a Ladies

Home Journal for herself, several spools of different-colored thread, a big bar of Ivory soap and some Pepsodent toothpaste. As a very special treat, she'd bought Pauline a bottle of Coca Cola. It was still cold, and Pauline had gulped it greedily. It had been so long since she'd had pop! She had the burps for a good half-hour afterwards.

Standing before the mirror, Pauline smiled at Mama and let her fasten the new ribbon in her hair with a bobby pin. She was a big girl now, nearly as tall as Mama, and growing more independent everyday. But as much as she liked to do things on her own, she knew she'd never be too old for Mama to brush her hair. Even though her light brown hair was cut in a plain, pageboy style that didn't quite reach her shoulders, when Mama ran the soft bristles of the hairbrush through it, she imagined she had long, luxurious, golden locks like Rapunzel.

"There! Now look." Mama had finished her work.

Pauline peered at herself in the mirror. Her hair looked shiny and healthy, the ribbon adding a touch of style to her image.

"Thank you, Mama," she said. "I love it."

Mama beamed and gave Pauline's shoulders a little squeeze.

Looking at Mama's reflection, Pauline thought she could see a change in her. Mama wasn't the type to fuss over her own appearance. It didn't seem to bother her that she had to wear the same couple of dresses, day after day. The closest thing to an accessory she owned, was the apron Poppa had bought her. She had carefully embroidered her initials on the pocket in a pretty, rose-colored thread. Her hair was always worn up in a loose bun; not for style, but to keep it out of her face while she did housework. Today, even though she wore it in the same fashion, it looked like she'd gone to great lengths to ensure that not a hair was out

of place. Pauline told herself it must be because Mama had
wanted to look nice when she went shopping.

There was something else she noticed. Pauline thought
she detected a hint of healthy color in Mama's normally
pale cheeks. On a typical weekday, Mama's brow was
laced with sweat from the exertion of ironing, washing and
cooking. But today her face looked relaxed and fresh-
scrubbed, even *younger*. Now that Pauline thought about it,
Mama hadn't been doing much housework lately. It wasn't
that she'd become lazy; but she'd never quite gotten back
to her old, back-breaking regimen once all the relatives left
the house. Maybe the fact that she was getting more rest
accounted for this transformation in Mama.

The more Pauline thought about it, she realized that the
change had been happening all along, although it had been
so subtle, so gradual, that it was easy to miss at first. But
now Pauline could see that Walter's death had changed
Mama dramatically, only not in the negative way the family
had predicted it would.

When she'd finally snapped out of her grieving trance,
Mama was no longer the submissive housewife she'd
always been. She didn't listen to Poppa when he barked
orders at her. At first, they thought Mama was daydreaming
and didn't hear him. But it soon became clear that she was
purposely ignoring him. Things got done, but she did them
in her own time, whereas she used to get right to work the
second he told her to do something.

Her newfound defiance infuriated Poppa. One evening,
she failed to grant his request to bring him his slippers,
saying: "They're six feet away from you. You're closer."
She didn't so much as look up from her mending when she
spoke.

Pauline was in the middle of washing dishes when she
overheard this. She nearly dropped a bowl, she was so

dumbstruck at Mama's retort. She quickly crossed the floor and peeked through the doorway, dreading the ugly battle she knew was about to ensue.

Poppa's expression was stunned at first. A split second later, it was replaced by one of rage. He sprang from his chair and lunged at Mama, who froze in her rocking chair. Poppa grabbed her roughly by her arm, dragging her out of the chair. Her needle and thread, and the socks she'd been mending, fell out of her lap as he jerked her from her seat. Mama struggled to keep her footing as he pulled her across the floor, but she kept stumbling. Poppa pushed her down roughly, beside the spot where his slippers lay.

"You will do as I say!" he hollered. He was so angry that Pauline could see little drops of spit flying from his mouth as he yelled. "Bring me my slippers, woman!"

He took a heavy hand to the back of Mama's head. Pauline recoiled as if she'd been the one he'd hit. Mama would probably have a headache for days.

Poppa thundered back to his chair. As if it weighed nothing, he picked it up and banged it on the hardwood floor three times before sitting down again. From the kitchen doorway, Pauline's eyes darted nervously from one parent to the other. Poppa sat erect in his chair, his hands clutching the armrests. His stance reminded her of the famous statue of Abraham Lincoln. Only instead of an intelligent, noble face carved in marble, Poppa's expression was a twisted mask of near-insanity. His eyes flashed with fire as he scowled at Mama, who remained slumped on the floor, where he'd left her. He didn't blink once as he waited for her to get up.

In the doorway, Pauline dared not move. She wasn't even sure if *she* was safe at this point. She wished she could blend in with the wooden door frame. As much as she wanted to run to Mama, to see if she was alright, she thought it was a good idea not to attract attention to herself.

Mama was laying so still at first, that Pauline thought she'd been knocked out. In time, though, Mama propped herself up on one elbow. She stayed in that position for awhile, then sat up and took several long, deep breaths. Doing so seemed to help her regain her senses. She raised a hand to the back of her head and rubbed it. Moving like an arthritic old woman, Mama reached for the slippers that had sparked this latest fiasco, and held them in her lap, sneering at them as if they were the most vile objects on earth.

Mama stood, unsteady at first. Once she had her bearings, she turned and faced Poppa. Pauline expected to see tears in her eyes, after what had just happened. But Mama looked as far from the brink of tears as could be. Instead, her eyes were full of the same fire she'd seen in Poppa's eyes just a few minutes ago. For a fear-filled moment, Pauline thought that Mama was going to throw the slippers at him.

Please, don't! She'd thought, as if her mother could hear what she was thinking. *It'll make him madder. He'll hurt you even worse. Don't do it, Mama!*

Much to Pauline's relief, Mama didn't throw the slippers. She carried them, in slow motion, to Poppa. She stopped about a half-foot in front of his chair and stood there, regarding him with a queer mixture of pity and repugnance.

Rather than handing the slippers to him, she dropped them at his feet. The muscles in Poppa's right shoulder tensed, as if he were ready to throw a punch, but Mama didn't even flinch. Her calm demeanor seemed to take the wind out of Poppa's sails. He leaned back in his chair, just staring. The two of them reminded Pauline of the feral cats that roamed the woods. This was how they looked when they had a stare-down. It would last until one of the cats slunk away, predicting its own defeat. Other times, the stand-off wouldn't be broken until one feline pounced on the other, initiating a snarling, bloody battle. Mama walked away.

Poppa picked up his slippers and put them on. His face regained its typical, stoic composure. He turned on his precious radio, picked up the newspaper, and began rattling the pages. Mama retrieved her mending from where it had fallen on the floor, sat down in her rocking chair, and resumed her work. It was as though nothing had happened!

Pauline couldn't comprehend any of it. Had she ever seen anything more bizarre? She realized she was still clutching the wet dishrag in her hand and remembered the soapy dishes that waited for her. She trudged over to the sink and finished the job as quickly as possible. That night, she put herself to bed, without saying "good night" to Mama or Poppa.

CHAPTER FIFTEEN

That knock-down-drag out fight was the first of many such incidents. Mama's defiance didn't wane; she continued to bestir Poppa's ire. Despite his violent retaliation, her insolence remained consistent. Poppa couldn't adjust to this bold stranger living under his roof.

Early on, his typical response to Mama's flippant remarks were slaps and angry cuss words. This was no different from the way he'd always handled things. What changed, was Mama's reaction. She no longer cowered or cried like she used to, begging for mercy as his fists pounded her tender, perpetually-bruised skin. Nor did she fight back. She simply turned the other cheek. If Poppa slammed her into a wall, she'd wait for her head to stop spinning, then smooth her dress and calmly walk away. No matter what names he called her or what he threatened to do to her, Mama didn't cry.

Poppa grew frustrated. For the first time, Pauline realized that there was more to her father's game than just being the "man of the house," whom nobody dared disobey. He needed to hear Mama's screams, to see her tears and to know she was in pain, in order to feel powerful. He was just as addicted to these things as he was to alcohol. Otherwise, it wasn't worth his while. He'd never known any woman to behave the way Mama was acting now.

Pauline could tell that Mama had figured this out too. As much as she infuriated him when she fought back with sharp words of her own, it was her stubborn silence and her non-reaction to his abuse that really drove Poppa nuts. He might as well be picking a fight with a wall. There was no fun in it for him anymore. Mama was wise to his game now, and, although Poppa might not know it, she was winning.

Thinking back, Pauline realized that this strategy was probably what saved *her* from the same fate her mother and brother had suffered. She could only recall Poppa hitting her two or three times in her life, when she'd done something that truly warranted a spanking. But never had she been subjected to the beatings that sometimes left Mama and Walter barely able to stand.

It's because I didn't cry, Pauline realized, as she watched the transition in her parents' relationship. Maybe she'd shed some tears the first time, but thereafter, she'd just freeze up, her body stiff as a board when Poppa took his belt to her. She was too scared to cry, even though it hurt. Her lack of reaction had caused Poppa to set his sights on the other two, who couldn't control their emotions.

The days went by in this surreal fashion for weeks. Pauline became aware of a mounting tension that was almost suffocating. She found it next to impossible to concentrate on her homework. For the first time in her life, her grades began to drop.

At suppertime, sitting between her parents, Pauline felt vulnerable. She was afraid that at any second, one of them would open fire on the other. And there she was, right in the middle of things. She was prepared to dive under the table in an instant, and make a beeline for the door before she could get caught in the crossfire.

At night, as she lay in bed, Pauline kept her ears open,

listening for any little sound that might indicate trouble. In the worst case, should Mama and Poppa appear to be in a life-threatening battle, Pauline was prepared to make a run for it. As much as she would want to stay and help Mama, she knew that the two of them, even together, weren't strong enough to win a fight with Poppa. Whatever might happen, she was determined to get out, unscathed. She wished they had a telephone in case of an emergency, but alas, their finances didn't allow them the luxury. If were able to get a hold of the keys to the Ford, she *might* be able to drive it into town, but she didn't think she should risk it. Pauline would have to rely on her wits and her fast feet to save herself and Mama.

But in the end, I couldn't, could I? she asked herself now. *I thought I was so smart, but here I am, and Mama is gone now, too..*

Tears streamed down Pauline's face as she remembered. She held the ribbon in the palm of her outstretched hand, like an offering to an invisible, unappeasable God. She did not see the torrents of rain that pummeled the window pane, nor the lightning flashes that lit up the sky like an out-of-control fireworks display. She saw a different scene altogether; the one that she'd viewed through the kitchen doorway on the last afternoon Mama had been alive.

She and Mama had been making bread to go with dinner. In between separating eggs, sifting flour and rolling out dough, they took time to comment on the changing scenery outside. For the first time in months, they were able to see patches of bare ground where the snow had melted. It was still chilly, but the promise of spring was most definitely on the horizon. They agreed that spring was the best season of all.

Looking at the bare branches of the trees, framed like a

painting by the windowsill, Pauline found it hard to believe that in just a few weeks, there would be green buds on all of them. Robins and bluebirds would twitter in the branches, talking to one another as they built the nests where their babies would hatch. As cheerful a scenario as this was, it made Pauline feel sad that Walter wouldn't be there to share it with her. He would have started school the following fall; a year later than most children, because of his health problems. But he would have caught up in no time, if he'd only had the chance…

It was a Saturday, and Poppa was home. He had been restless all day, finding little projects to do around the house. He oiled door hinges that barely squeaked. He made a shim for the one leg of the kitchen table that had always been shorter than the others. He even repaired a stepstool he'd broken during a drunken tantrum. If he hadn't been within earshot all day, Mama would have said Poppa had a bad case of "the fidgets." He made them nervous with his constant going back and forth, but they tried their best to ignore him. Once he'd run out of things to do, Poppa sat in his armchair and smoked his pipe for a while, lost in thought. At some point, he slipped off without a word. Pauline recalled looking up from the mixing bowl and noticing that his chair was empty. She figured that he was in the bathroom and went about her work.

"What are you doing?!" Mama's voice startled Pauline so much that she dropped the spoon she'd been stirring with. She tried to grab hold of it, but it fell to the floor with a clang. At first she thought that *she* had done something wrong. But Mama brushed past her, out of the kitchen and into the living room.

"What do you think you are doing?" Mama repeated. Poppa had reappeared, with a small bundle of clothing tucked under his arm.

"I'm doin' what *you* oughta be doin'," Poppa snapped. "It doesn't take the two of you to make bread. Pauline can do that by herself. I'm cleanin' house."

"What are you going to do with those?" Mama reached for the clothes, but he pulled them away just before she could touch them.

"What's it matter?" Poppa asked. "We don't need 'em anymore. There's other folks that do."

Pauline realized that the clothing Poppa held had belonged to Walter. She spotted the dark brown cardigan that had been so baggy on Walter's small frame, and the peppermint-stripe pajamas that he'd worn every day during the last weeks of his life.

"You aren't throwing those away!" Mama made another grab for the clothes. Poppa had anticipated the move, and quickly transferred them to his other arm. He backed away from Mama with a smirk that challenged her to try again.

"Didn't say I was throwin' 'em away," Poppa said. "Said there's other folks that could use 'em. They're just collectin' dust layin' 'round here. No sense in that. Figure we could donate 'em to someone in the church, considerin' all they done for us when..."

"YOU aren't the one who made those clothes!" Mama was shouting now. "YOU aren't the one who spent 16 hours giving birth to that boy, and the better part of six years nursing him when he was in ill health. All you ever did was hurt him!"

Poppa was so stunned by her outburst that he allowed her to swipe Walter's old clothes from the crook of his arm. She clutched them tight to her bosom like a sack of hundred dollar bills.

"You *won't* give these away!" she insisted, even though Poppa was making no move to confiscate the clothes. His arms hung at his sides. For once, he was speechless.

Mama, on the other hand, appeared to be having a breakdown of sorts. She was choking on her own sobs. After weeks of being non-emotional, her tears overflowed now. Her eyes flashed with the defiance of a wild animal. Even more frightening was the ferocious manner in which she held on to Walter's clothes. It was as though she were protecting a live baby, and not a bundle of worn-out clothing.

From her vantage point in the kitchen, Pauline's lower lip trembled and she had to chew on it to keep from crying, too. She could see that something had snapped in Mama's mind. Had Poppa finally driven her crazy?

"Mary! Calm down! You're making somethin' out of nothin'!" Poppa scolded her, but the normal gruffness in his voice wasn't there.

"I... am.. NOT!" Mama was hysterical. "A little boy *died!* Don't tell me that's '*nothing*'!"

"I didn't say.." Poppa held up both hands defensively.

"Yes, you did." Mama stood her ground. "You did! And YOU, of all people, should know better."

"Mary…" Poppa's voice was stern now, warning her to push the topic any farther. His no-nonsense demeanor had returned. He rolled up his sleeves and advanced towards Mama, who began walking backwards. Pauline marveled at how Mama instinctively knew when to turn, to avoid bumping into the furniture.

"Don't even speak my name!" Mama screamed.

Pauline's jaw dropped. She had never heard Mama scream, other than in pain. This was the explosion Pauline knew had been coming. She wanted to run to Mama, grab her by the hand and pull her back to reality. If she didn't act fast, the mother that she loved would disappear forever, trapped inside this crazy person. Now was the time to play out the scenes she'd rehearsed in her head at least a hundred times. It was her chance to be a heroine.

Go! Run out the door, all the way to town, she instructed herself. *Get help, fast! You can't stop Poppa yourself!*

But fear glued her to the floor.

"You had no right!" Mama cried, even as Poppa gripped her by the arms and shook her. "You had no right to treat him the way you did! He didn't deserve it!"

"Shut up, woman!" Poppa barked. "I didn't treat him no different than my father treated me!"

"I don't believe it!" Mama half-screamed, half-sobbed. "You always *knew*, from the second he was born and you first laid eyes on him. All his life, you took it out on him. You took it out on *me*, too, and I accepted it because I thought I deserved it. But Walter didn't deserve it! He was a baby! He was innocent, Bill. He didn't understand!"

"I told you to SHUT UP!" Poppa was hitting her now, smacking her first on one side of her head, then the other.

Pauline raised her hands to her mouth to muffle a scream of her own. In all her life, she'd never seen Poppa this mad.

"I've 'shut up' for too long!" Mama shrieked. "I've had enough! I'm taking Pauline and we're leaving."

"Leaving?!" Poppa snorted. "You've lost your mind! Where would you go?"

"Oh, I'd find someplace." Mama pushed his hands off her and moved back. "You underestimate me. I've lost one child. I will not lose my daughter too."

"You're crazy," Poppa accused, kicking over Mama's rocking chair. "You need to be in a crazy house."

"No!" Mama interrupted him. "I'm perfectly sane. You're the one who's crazy!"

"How dare you talk to me that way?" Poppa shouted.

"Listen to yourself! You say you're gonna leave? How? You ain't got no money. You ain't even got no bags packed. How can you leave, you silly bitch? You can't even drive. You can't do anything. And I tell you, you try and take that kid outta here, you'll be in big trouble, woman."

"No." Mama narrowed her eye and pointed an accusing finger at her husband. "You've got it all wrong. You're the one who's in trouble."

"Trouble? Me?" Poppa shrugged with exaggerated innocence. "What are you talkin' about? You're the one about to become a kidnapper."

"But YOU are something much worse," Mama yelled. "You are a MURDERER!"

Mama screamed the word so loud, Pauline thought it must have resonated through the miles of woods that surrounded the house. She didn't even have time to absorb the truth of Mama's accusation when the fighting began again.

Poppa swung at Mama, but she ducked, dropping to her knees. She sprang back up, ready to take him on.

"You knew exactly what you were doing when you locked him out," she continued. "You wished Walter dead from the day he was born. Even before he was born, you *suspected*. You've always suspected. You might never have said it, but you didn't have to. You've shown me, with every slap, with every curse, with every bruise you've ever given me."

"You're about to get a lot worse than a bruisin'!" Poppa threatened. He took hold of her wrists. She dropped down and tried to tried to wrench herself away from him, but he easily dragged her to her feet.

"You speak to me face to face!" he yelled, his face an inch from Mama's. "You're beating all around the bush.

Just say it, Mary, and be done with it. Say what neither one of us has said for six years. If you just say it right now, it'll be over and done with. I promise."

There was dead silence for what seemed like forever. Pauline thought that time had stopped altogether, but then she heard the tick-ticking of Poppa's watch in his shirt pocket.

"Walter..." Mama spoke in a shaky voice.

"What?!?" Poppa urged her on with a jab of his elbow in her ribs. "What about Walter?"

"He wasn't yours!" Mama screamed. Her face was scarlet. Her chest heaved, as she tried to bring her hysteria under control. "There! Are you happy now? I said it!"

"You whore!" Poppa smacked her on the side of her head and she reeled to the floor.

"You promised!" she wailed, sounding like a little girl. "You lied to me! You promised that if I told you the truth, it'd be 'over and done with.' That's means you're letting me go! I'm leaving. I can't take it anymore. All this living in fear, and pretending that nothing's wrong, when *everything* is wrong. And it's no good for Pauline to grow up this way, either."

"Leave Pauline out of this!"

At the sound of her name on Poppa's lips, Pauline trembled. She hugged herself tight, but she couldn't stop shaking. Her teeth chattered together. Even though it was a warm day, she felt as cold as Walter must have during that nightmarish winter storm. Her legs felt like melting icicles. She wondered how much longer they could hold her up.

"There's a *big* difference between *your* little Walter and *my* Pauline," Poppa said. He poked Mama in the chest to punctuate each word. "Pauline is my flesh and blood. And Walter was a little bastard."

"Don't talk about my son that way!"

Mama jumped up at him, a whirlwind of swinging fists. She caught Poppa off-guard, managing to clock him in the eye. He grunted and grabbed for her, but she ducked, then bounced back to her feet with the agility of a girl half her age.

"Come on, baby. We're leaving!" Mama rushed towards Pauline.

Something happened then, that Pauline would never be able to explain to herself. She saw Mama rushing towards her, but it *wasn't* Mama. Gone was the mother who had cooed lullabies to her, long past the age when she should have indulged the girl in such childish things. There was no trace of the woman who'd patiently taught her to sew and to knit, nor of the friend who'd spent so many quiet, happy hours sitting with her, reading the Bible and helping her with her homework.

Even physically, Mama had changed. The arms that had hugged her every night before bed, and comforted her after hundreds of Poppa's blow-ups, were now the flailing tendons of a monster. The fingers that had lovingly wiped away her children's tears, now seemed like ugly, twisted talons. Worst of all, were Mama's eyes. All Pauline had ever seen in them was love, wisdom and patience. But now she found herself looking into the eyes of a stranger. The terrifying apparition that was running towards her was not her mother. It was a madwoman.

"Poppa! Help Me!" Pauline screamed, finding her voice at last.

The three words she never should have said, or Mama might be alive today. She regretted them as soon as they were spoken, for that simple sentence stopped Mama in her tracks. The mask of lunacy melted back into the soft, familiar face of her mother. The realization that she'd so badly frightened her only living child hit Mama hard. She immediately tried to apologize through a bout of sobs, but it came out as gibberish.

Frustrated by her inability to get the words out, Mama became hysterical again. She pawed at Pauline like a blind woman, unable to see clearly though her tears. Pauline backed away, afraid of her mother for the first time in her life. Just as Mama's fingers were closing on her sleeve, Poppa yanked her away by the arm.

Pauline crawled away, taking cover beneath the kitchen table She was far enough away from the insanity that was happening in the living room, but still close enough to see what was going on. From her makeshift shelter, Pauline sent a half-hearted prayer up to Heaven, begging God to return Mama to her rightful mind. But as she watched the war unfold, and heard her mother emit grunts and noises that were nothing like words, she relinquished her last shred of hope.

Pauline found her mind drifting back to a time when she couldn't have been more than three years old. She was wearing a white flannel nightgown with blue daisies on it, and she was trying very hard to learn her bedtime prayers for Mama. She didn't understand what all of the words meant at the time, but she knew they must be very important, for it made Mama so happy when she recited them. Side by side, they'd get down on their knees beside the bed, heads bowed and fingers folded, and talk to God. She couldn't remember when or why they had stopped this ritual; she'd forgotten all about it until now.

Witnessing the wrestling match that was taking place in the living room, Pauline wondered if Mama could even remember The Lord's Prayer, in the state she was in. As she watched her mother crawling on her hands and knees, Pauline started reciting it herself.

"Our Father, who art in Heaven..." she began

whispering out loud.

No sooner had the words crossed her lips, when Mama spotted her in her hiding place. She moved towards Pauline with such speed, there was no time to get out of the way.

Pauline screamed. She tried to stand up, bumped her head hard on the underside of the table and fell back down. She knew she was going to faint. She remembered feeling dizzy, and having just enough time to worry that she might wake up with an ugly "goose egg." Then everything went black.

She couldn't have been out for very long. She awoke to find herself still under the kitchen table. Slowly, cautiously, she raised her throbbing head. Her focus was blurry at first. Pauline closed her eyes tightly and counted to ten before opening them again. She saw floating red spots. It took a minute for her vision to clear.

It was the utter silence that brought her completely back to her senses. The ruckus that had been taking place moments ago had ceased. Where were Mama and Poppa? Pauline started to venture out from under the table to investigate. Before she got very far, she heard something that stopped her cold.

She hadn't awakened to perfect silence after all. Compared to the commotion of a few minutes ago, it was quiet. But as she listened harder, she heard an unusual, soft noise that she couldn't quite identify. Yet, something about it made her skin crawl.

Her heartbeat increased. Danger's presence was palpable. Pauline wanted nothing more than to lay down under the table and go back to sleep. She had the worst headache ever. But that was just an excuse, she knew, to avoid facing whatever was in the living room.

CHAPTER SIXTEEN

Pauline inched along on her elbows. Lying flat on her belly, she made her way to the far end of the table, so she was laying under the exact spot where Walter used to sit. Either Mama or Poppa had recently moved his chair to a corner of the kitchen, so nothing was blocking her way. Pauline pulled herself ahead a little more, until half of her body stuck out from beneath the table. Now she was able to peer through the doorway. Although her every brain cell was warning her not to, Pauline looked anyway.

Mama had been the source of the noise she'd heard. There was a weird, gurgling sound coming from her throat. She and Poppa were no more than ten feet away from Pauline. They were standing face to face. This immediately struck Pauline as odd, because Poppa was nearly a foot taller than Mama. Was Mama standing on something?

When she looked down to see if this was the case, Pauline's mind refused, at first, to accept what she saw. Mama's feet were dangling inches above the floor. The reason she and Poppa were face-to-face was because he was holding her in mid-air by her neck.

A scream stuck in Pauline's throat, followed by the burning sensation of stomach acid. She forced it back down and stifled the cry that had nearly escaped. She wanted to look away, but she couldn't even close her eyes. They were riveted to the macabre scene that was unfolding in the next room.

Mama's hands were on top of Poppa's, her short fingernails digging into his flesh. It was a futile attempt. She'd managed to make a few small scratches that drew dots of blood, but that wasn't enough to deter him. And there was certainly no hope of her small, feminine hands prying his strong fingers from her neck.

The struggle must have been going on for as long as she'd been unconscious, because Pauline could tell that it was almost over. Clearly, most of the fight was already gone from Mama's spirit. Her body was even weaker. Little by little, Mama's grip loosened, until, defeated, her arms fell limp at her sides. Her feet, which had been searching in vain for the ground, were finally still. Once again, there was no sound except for the ticking of Poppa's watch.

It's over. He can't hurt her anymore. Pauline was shocked that she felt a sense of relief.

But the worst *wasn't* over, Pauline realized, as she took another look at her mother. Horror gripped her when she saw Mama's face. It was almost unrecognizable now. Her skin had turned a purplish hue, and her eyes were bulging so that they appeared ready to pop out of their sockets. Her tongue protruded from her mouth. Pauline thought back on all the times when Mama had scolded her and Walter for sticking their tongues out at each other. "Rude" and "disgusting" were a couple of the adjectives her mother had used to describe such behavior. She couldn't help thinking that Mama would be ashamed if she could see herself now.

Mama is dead.

Pauline tried to push the thought out of her mind, but she couldn't. She saw it, like a newspaper headline in boldface type: **MAMA IS DEAD.** She saw it written in chalk on the blackboard at school. It was etched in a cemetery stone by the church; drawn with a stick in the snow: **MAMA IS DEAD**. She visualized the three words in all possible combinations her head.

While Pauline understood the meaning of this sentence, she didn't feel like it pertained to *her*. It was as though she were reading about someone else; an unfortunate little girl in a fictional book she'd checked out of the library. Her brain's defense mechanism had already kicked in. It was hard at work, protecting her sanity by suppressing the memory, even as it was still happening. But deep down, Pauline knew the truth. She would never forget what she'd seen that day. The pictures were permanently engraved in her mind, although they were buried layers upon layers beneath the surface. But not forever. No amount of years, lies or distractions could keep it from eventually bubbling back up to the top.

"Mama, where are you?" Pauline called in the dark attic. "Oh, what did Poppa do with you?"

Her mother should have been buried next to Walter. For all Pauline knew, Mama's body could be hidden somewhere in this house, maybe in the basement. The thought made her shudder.

The blue hair ribbon was wet in her hand, covered with sweat. Pauline put it under her pillow, where Mark had been. It just hurt her too much to look at it right now. She wiped her hands on the skirt of her dress.

Mama's dress.

Suddenly, Pauline recalled the prayer she had said on that day she'd awakened to find Poppa looking at her so strangely.

"If they're with You, send me a sign," she repeated now. "You *did*."

Trembling, she retrieved the ribbon and clutched it to her chest. The tears that fell now were not tears of grief or mourning, but tears of joy. For Pauline now had no doubt that God had, indeed, sent her the sign she'd asked for.

The ribbon! It was the ribbon! she thought with a smile.

She laughed out loud at the fact that the messenger He had chosen, had been a *rat*, of all things. The aching in her heart dissipated, replaced by a sort of warmth that she hadn't felt in a long time. It was the same feeling she used to get when Mama brushed her hair; or when a sick Walter smiled gratefully up at her from his bed as she read him a story. Plain and simple, it was the feeling of knowing she was loved.

CHAPTER SEVENTEEN

Something shattered the peace of the moment. Pauline cocked her head and listened. Had she just heard something, above the commotion of the thunderstorm? She listened carefully. Yes, she was sure of it. Something was moving in the house, behind the locked door. Between the top of the stairs and the bedroom door, there was a small room that served as storage space. It was chock full of old trunks and boxes of junk left behind after her grandparents died. Whatever Poppa's sisters didn't want- mostly musty, old-fashioned clothing, books and decades' worth of newspapers- had been packed up and lugged up to the attic. Right now, it sounded like somebody was rummaging through those boxes.

Pauline backed away from the door, cautious. She hadn't heard Poppa's footsteps coming up the stairs. But who else could it be? Her next guess was that it might be the rat- perhaps many of them- making the racket, but she quickly dismissed that thought. The noise was most definitely made by something larger than a rodent. It sounded as though somebody was sifting through papers and things in box after box, like they were searching for something, and tossing items onto the floor as they went along. It *had* to be Poppa. But why on earth would he be digging through the boxes now, in the middle of a thunderstorm?

A loud *THUD* made her jump. Something heavy had been knocked over. She put her ear right up to the door and listened. Nothing. A few seconds later, Pauline heard Poppa's feet on the stairs. Only, they were *ascending* the staircase, not going down. Pauline was alarmed by this. Was there an intruder in the house?

Poppa's key jabbed away at the keyhole, finding its mark after several drunken attempts. Pauline scrambled onto the mattress, afraid he'd yell at her for not being in bed. The door swung open and he stood there, a dark silhouette looming in the threshold. He shone a lantern directly on Pauline's face. She was temporarily blinded by the bright light. She squinted and held a hand in front of her eyes in protest.

"What are you doing?" they asked each other in unison. Under normal circumstances, Pauline might have giggled at the coincidence, but the moment was overshadowed by apprehension.

"I heard a commotion up here," Poppa said in a somber monotone.

"Me too," Pauline whispered.

"What was it?" Poppa inquired.

"I thought it was you," said Pauline.

"I was downstairs," Poppa stated.

"I was in bed," Pauline lied. "I thought I heard someone going through boxes in there." She pointed to the dark area beyond the door. "And then something dropped."

"Somebody's in here." Poppa's eyes narrowed with paranoia.

"I'm scared." Pauline hugged the pillow to her body.

"Stay here." Poppa ordered.

He picked up the sharp-pointed stick that he'd given Pauline to kill the rat, and cautiously stepped into the other room. She knew he was trying to be quiet, but that was next to impossible in this old house. Every time a floorboard creaked beneath his foot, Pauline cringed. At any moment, she was sure an axe-wielding maniac would jump out from behind the stacks of boxes and chop both of them to pieces.

"Looks like this here storm got us spooked," Poppa called out. There was a nervous laugh in his voice that told Pauline everything must be OK. But still, he sounded like he'd been quite frightened himself. "Come see."

Reluctantly, Pauline left the safe haven of her mattress and, still clutching her pillow, padded towards the sound of Poppa's voice. He stood by an old bookshelf. He directed the lantern's light so that she could see what had happened. One of the shelves had completely rotted, caving in under the weight of the books it held. The heavy tomes had toppled against a box of yellowed newspapers, which had, in turn, tumbled to the floor.

"I'll take care of the mess tomorrow," Poppa said. "Not now. It's late and I'm tuckered out. Get yourself back to your room."

Pauline trotted ahead of Poppa, feeling as relieved as he sounded. When they entered the bedroom, something else caught her father's attention.

"Is *that* what you were so afraid of?"

Now that the "danger" had passed, Poppa's voice had taken on the familiar, mocking tone that Pauline hated so much. She looked to where he was pointing.

There, looking up at them in the glow of the candle's light, was the rat. It stood motionless, except for the constant twitching of its little nose. Pauline found it hard to believe that just a few days ago, she'd been afraid of the animal. She hadn't decided yet whether the rat knew what he was doing when he brought her the hair ribbon, or if he had simply acted under God's guidance, without understanding his mission. She did know she was grateful, and she felt a fondness for the creature.

"I'm not afraid of him anymore," Pauline said.

"No?" Poppa sounded skeptical. "Here, then."

He shoved the stick into Pauline's hands, then crossed his arms across his chest and grinned at her expectantly.

Pauline stared at the stick as if she'd never seen one before. She felt stupid for not understanding what Poppa wanted her to do. She looked up at him questioningly.

"Go ahead," Poppa said. "Show me you're not afraid. Prove it."

It slowly registered in Pauline's mind what her father expected. He wanted her to use the stick to kill the rat. To *murder* it!

He wants me to be like him! Pauline thought.

Anger welled up inside her. Did Poppa really think that she was anything like him? All the years she'd been alive, she'd tried to please him. She'd strived to be as good as possible. Against her own judgment, she had played the role of the "little woman" to make Poppa happy. While Pauline fantasized about growing up to be a doctor as well as a housewife, all such dreams had to be kept under wraps. Up to this moment, she'd thought she'd succeeded in pleasing her father. She'd thought that even if Poppa didn't actually *love* her, at least he must be proud of her. That belief was shattered now.

She glared at him. Had *this* been Poppa's motive in keeping her alive all this time; to turn her into a female, junior version of himself? Was this some kind of initiation, to prove that she was, in fact, her father's daughter? Did he expect her to succeed where Walter had failed? She cared nothing about winning his respect now.

She was about to flat-out refuse him, when she remembered what he'd said about moving to Minnesota. If she didn't obey him now, he very well might change his mind. She didn't want to mess up what might be her only chance at getting away from Poppa. Where she'd go and how she'd survive, she had no idea, but she'd make her way somehow.

Pauline hadn't realized until this moment how desperately she wanted out of Adams, and out of The Old Homestead. With Momma and Walter gone, there was nobody left who loved her. Her friends must have long since forgotten her by now, and the Aunts and Uncles who'd been so helpful after Walter's death had drifted away, getting back to their own lives in faraway towns. She decided that starting over in a new place would be better than trying to pick up the pieces here. Was obeying Poppa the only way out?

She turned the stick around and 'round in her hands, looking from it to the rat. If it knew its life was in danger, the animal showed no sign of it. He was as carefree as could be, dawdling in the lantern light, regarding the two humans with dumb curiosity.

"No."

Pauline's voice was strong and resolute. She was surprised at how grown-up she sounded. Her stance could not be mistaken for the squeamishness of a frightened little girl.

Even Poppa, still slightly intoxicated, could see a stubbornness in his daughter's eyes which had not been there before. It struck a nerve that hadn't been irritated in quite some time. Not since...

"You're just like your mother," Poppa said in a voice that was just above a whisper. The glaze of alcohol disappeared from his eyes. He looked, all at once, keenly sober. "Just like her."

He put down the lantern and they locked eyes. Pauline

regretted her objection, but it was too late to take it back.

Pauline was suddenly aware that a dark, invisible presence had slipped into the room, like a sneaky black cat. The intangible enemy took sides with Poppa. Pauline was outnumbered.

Although she was terrified, she had also become aware of another emotion; the fury that burned inside her. It had been there, smoldering, for a long time, but only now was she able to recognize and understand it. She'd never been allowed to be angry before. Ten years worth of bottled-up feelings were now spilling their contents.

Standing across from her drunken father, her head squeezed by a vise of decisions she didn't want to make, Pauline was incensed by the sheer *unfairness* of it all. She mourned the three wasted lives she had witnessed: Walter's, Mama's, and now, her own. Why hadn't God helped her when she called on Him? Why had He taken her mother and brother? Pauline chided herself for believing that the hair ribbon was a divine sign that her loved ones were safe in Heaven. Maybe there was no such place. Her hopes had been raised for nothing. Somehow she had failed God's test; now she felt as though the Devil was mocking her now, for being so foolish.

Poppa took a step towards her, and she took two steps back, unconsciously raising the stick to her chest. Poppa snorted.

"What are you going to do with that?" he sneered. When Pauline didn't answer, he grabbed it and tried to wrench it out of her hands.

They struggled in a father-versus-daughter tug-of-war. Poppa had an obvious advantage, but Pauline, sensing that her life was on the line, fought with all the strength she had. Back and forth, they went, in what must have looked like an Indian tribal dance. But instead of beckoning rain or a fruitful harvest, Pauline felt like they were summoning Armageddon. When she gazed up at Poppa's livid face, she believed that the gates of Hell had, in fact, opened up.

Poppa let go of the stick. Pauline was caught by surprise and stumbled backwards. Before she could recover her footing, Poppa picked her up and threw her across the room. She crashed hard against the wall and slid to the floor with a moan.

Stunned and sore, Pauline heard Poppa's footsteps pounding towards her, but she couldn't move. Her spine throbbed with pain as he loomed over her, regarding her with a crooked smile. Lying on her side, Pauline instinctively curled her body around the stick when Poppa reached down to take it out of her hands, yet she didn't resist him when he pulled it away.

When she looked up, she expected to see Poppa holding the pointed stick high over his head. She was positive he intended to stab her, just as she'd been instructed to impale the rodent. But she was wrong. Poppa held the stick at his side. He rubbed his bearded chin with one finger, the way he did when he was debating his strategy in a poker game. Pauline felt chilled, imagining the deadly scenarios that must be running through his head. Was Poppa really trying to make up his mind about what to do to her, or did he just want to prolong her agony?

Her question would never be answered. For, just as he raised the stick above his head and Pauline braced herself for its deadly impact, Poppa cried out in pain.

"God damn it!" he shouted.

Pauline took advantage of the moment to get out of his way. Her back still hurt too much to stand up, but she was able to scramble away from him, crab-walking into the corner. She looked to see what it was that had caused Poppa to cry out. When she saw, she was astounded.

The rat had bitten Poppa on the ankle. In fact, it had *attached* itself to him, its sharp teeth drawing blood, as it hung on him like a leech. Poppa was trying to shake it off, but he couldn't. He spat out a string of curse words, hopping about in agony. Then, gathering his wits, he remembered he had the stick in his hand. He used it to hit the animal in the head. A couple of hearty whacks did the job, and the disoriented creature finally let go, staggering in a crooked path towards Pauline, as if it thought she might be able to help. It hadn't gone more than a few pathetic steps when Poppa speared it.

Pauline let out a long, shrill wail, mourning the death of the creature she'd come to regard as a friend. Little drops of its blood spattered on her dress. Not thinking, she tried to wipe it off and then gagged when it got on her hands.

Poppa, now free to resume his original mission, turned his attentions back to her. He threw the stick aside.

"I'll kill you with my bare hands," he vowed.

With nothing to stop him now, Poppa slogged towards her, limping on his injured leg. Blood trickled down his ankle, dripping down the side of his shoe as he approached. Pauline noticed it, then spotted something else, behind Poppa. It was something that terrified her much more than the madman who was about to wring her neck. She tried to find her voice to warn him.

Before she could get out more than a squeak, he had pulled her to her feet by the collar of her dress. She heard the material rip in his angry hands. He shook her so violently, Pauline felt like her brain was rattling around in her head. He reminded her more of a bear, on the verge of tearing its prey apart.

"Poppa..." Pauline tried to get his attention, but her voice was useless.

Poppa squeezed her arms until she thought her bones

would break. He lifted her, pinned her against the wall and held her there, with her feet dangling no more than an inch off the ground. Pauline knew it was a matter of seconds before his hands would be squeezing her neck. He was killing Mama all over again.

Looking into his eyes, Pauline was pretty sure he'd let go of any shred of sanity that might have remained. She might not be able to get through to him. But she had to try, before...

"Poppa, behind you," she managed to squeak. Then, in full voice: "LOOK BEHIND YOU!"

Suspicion clouded Poppa's mad eyes. Still holding his daughter in a viselike grip, he cast a wary glance over his shoulder, sure it was a trick.

"Shit!"

Poppa dropped Pauline. The girl hadn't lying. When he'd thrown the stick- with the dead rat still attached to it- across the room, it had knocked over Pauline's candle. The flame had caught the mattress on fire. He made a mad dash to try and get it under control.

"Jesus Christ!"

Poppa looked around in desperation. He spotted an old, dusty throw rug on the floor. He grabbed it and made a vain attempt to beat the flames out. The rug caught on fire, too, burning quickly, because it was so dry. Poppa yowled in pain as the fast-moving flames bit his fingertips. He threw the rug down and stomped on it. It burned almost as quickly as paper.

This can't be happening! Pauline thought, watching the scene unfold with disbelief. It was like a deadly chain of dominoes toppling each other over, as one thing after another went wrong.

Poppa was doing a wild dance, and at first Pauline thought her father was trying still trying to stamp out the flames as they spread. But she realized, with revulsion, that Poppa was on fire. It had caught one of his shoe laces first. The tiny flame, barely bigger than a spark, climbed a criss-cross path up the laces, then jumped onto the cuff of his pant leg. Now Poppa had a bigger problem.

Meanwhile, the mattress had become a roaring bonfire. Pauline was surprised, in a detached sort of way, at how quickly the fire was spreading. She remained where she was, making no attempt to escape.

Poppa, on the other hand, was panicking. He backed away from the burning mattress, hopping on the leg that wasn't on fire. With both hands, he batted at the flames that were consuming his trousers. His palms blistered, and he yelped in pain. Pauline thought of all the times those very hands had hit Walter and Mama. She felt no sympathy for Poppa now.

For a moment, it looked as though her father had gotten the best of the situation. He'd patted out the fire on his body. His left leg was a black, smoking mess, and Pauline wondered if she was looking at charred fabric or burnt skin. Judging from the awful smell, and from the agonized grimace on Poppa's face, Pauline decided it must be the latter. He groaned, and tried to lean against the wall. He fell down instead, and in doing so, sealed his fate. For when he went down, he crashed into the lantern that he'd placed beside the doorway. The glass shattered and kerosene splashed everywhere. The flame that had given the lamp its light jumped out at Poppa like a live animal. It pounced on his chest, then moved quickly to cover his entire upper body. He screamed, in a high-pitched voice that sounded like a woman's. In agony, he rose to his knees, his burning arms and hands outstretched. The fire paused at Poppa's neck, tickling his beard with lethal fingers. One last time, his eyes connected with Pauline's. Then, he made one final, useless plea.

"Oh, God! Please! *Nooo...*" he cried.

The flames leapt upwards, as if baited by his very breath, and engulfed his head. Pauline watched numbly; first as her father's hair burned away, then as his screaming face melted behind an orange curtain of fire. It was only after he'd pitched backwards, dead, that she started to think about her own situation.

She stood up slowly, rubbing her sore back. The intense heat threatened to overcome her. As the flames grew higher and crept closer to her, she was aware of the peril; but she wasn't afraid. The fire was soon just a few inches away, on either side of her.

Beyond the open door, in the other room, Pauline could see the silhouette of a man. This did not strike her as strange. She found herself smiling... *smiling!* in the midst of this death and destruction. Although she could not see his face, she knew that this man was her friend.

Ignoring all of her other surroundings, Pauline began walking towards him. She could hear pieces of the ceiling falling down behind her. To her left and right, the fire seemed to wait for her, closing in as soon as she'd passed. Ahead of her, the path remained clear. Not once did she feel she was in any danger, as she headed towards her rescuer. When Pauline was within a few feet of him, he reached his arms out to her.

Her pace increased to a run. She sprinted forward and leaped into his arms, hugging his neck. He gave her a reassuring squeeze before turning around and walking away from the advancing flames. She let him carry her away from the burning room, away from Poppa. She briefly worried that they might not be fast enough. What if the stairs...

"It's okay," the man said when he felt her body tense.

"Don't be afraid, Pauline."

She obeyed, resting her head on his broad shoulder. Smoke stung her nostrils and burned her eyes. She took too deep a breath, and the thick fumes made her cough uncontrollably. She had just started to gag, when the air cleared.

It was as though they had passed through a magic door. The smoke, the scorching heat, and the all-consuming flames that had threatened their lives just seconds ago, were gone.

Her head still buried in the chest of the mysterious man who held her, Pauline sensed the changes, but was afraid to open her eyes.

"It's okay." The man seemed to read her mind. His deep voice was reassuring. "Look."

CHAPTER EIGHTEEN

Pauline peeked out of the corner of her eye, still not convinced the nightmare was over. She thought she saw the sky. But how...? When she turned her face upwards, her jaw dropped in amazement.

She was looking at the bluest sky she'd ever seen, with not the slight smudge of a cloud. The sun was an 18-karat gold platter. It kissed her skin with a warmth she had missed during her months of confinement to the attic. The trees were in full bloom; their leaves a gorgeous Kelly green. She felt like she'd stepped into a gorgeous painting.

Pauline's practical mind kicked in. What she was seeing couldn't be real. There was no way they could have gotten out of her house without getting burned. Why didn't she hear fire trucks? It must have been a fireman who'd so bravely carried her out of the inferno. Except, she couldn't remember him taking her down the stairs. One minute, the fire was on their heels, and the next, they were here. But where was "here"?

She would make sure to thank the man who'd saved her life, just as soon as she figured out what had happened. She tried to look over his shoulder, to see what remained of her house. Was it still burning?

"Don't look." The man's voice was gentle but firm.

"Never look back."

She did as she was told. Instead she looked up, towards the sound of his voice. She wanted to see the face of her hero. The sun wouldn't let her. Its brilliance intensified almost tenfold, and she had to close her eyes immediately. All she'd caught was a shadowy glimpse, like a silhouette, of her rescuer. Even though she hadn't seen his features, Pauline felt as though she'd just gazed upon the most beautiful face on earth.

He set her down gently. Pauline was surprised to find that the pain in her back had gone away. She felt steady on her feet. Looking down, she marveled at the greenness of the grass. To her surprise and delight, she saw that little buttercups had sprung up among the blades. Why, buttercups had never grown in this yard before. Not like at their old place, by the railroad tracks, where they'd been abundant.

"Pauline!" a young voice called out to her.

She looked in the direction of the voice and froze. The scene before her was impossibly beautiful. And it was also just plain impossible.

She was not in the yard of the house where she'd lived for the past four years; that dark, isolated place in the woods. She was looking at their old "shack by the tracks," as Mama had nick-named it. Only, it looked nothing like she remembered it. The shack had been a dilapidated, make-do dwelling, far from a thing of beauty. But the little house had been all patched up and painted. The dull gray wood was now a bright, clean white, and the roof no longer sagged in. There was new glass in the windows, which were trimmed in cheerful red paint. The petunias that Mama had tended to with such care, were in full bloom on either side of the steps. Pauline recalled Poppa ripping them up by their roots during one of his drunken fits, but that unpleasant memory faded just as quickly as it had surfaced. Her eyes drank in the array of purples, pinks and reds of the flowers. How Mama would have loved to have seen her garden come back to life like this!

Pauline was even more amazed when she spotted the apple tree, in the small plot of land that had passed for their backyard. It had been healthy once, providing the family with tart, juicy treats every season. But disease had set in. The last time she'd seen the tree, its leaves had been covered with brown splotches, and there were ugly, dark scabs on the fruit. Now, by some miracle, the tree was thriving once again. Its branches were loaded with apples, bigger than they'd ever grown while she'd lived there. She would have thought it was a different tree altogether, but she recognized the particular branch that she used to sit on. She remembered practicing the songs she'd learned in music class, swinging her feet as she sang. Walter, who'd been just a toddler, would bat at her shoes, chortling, with a giant grin on his baby face. That familiar, crooked branch assured her that it was, without a doubt, the same tree.

She turned to ask the man who'd saved her life what was going on. He was gone.

Pauline felt a twinge of panic. Had he left her alone? Why would he walk off without saying a word? Why hadn't she heard him leave? Pauline's head swam with confusion.

The next thought that crossed her mind was that this house no longer belonged to her family. Therefore, wasn't she trespassing? She knew she ought to turn around and go, but she was more tempted to go and knock on the door. Maybe they had a telephone and she could call for help. Only who would believe the wild story she had to tell?

Pauline took a hesitant step towards the house. Thoughts of the fire were beginning to fade from her mind, replaced by a strong preoccupation with her old house. If she politely explained to the new owners that she used to live there, and complimented them on the beautiful work they'd done, might they be so kind as to show her the inside? Surely, they'd done just as many repairs to the living quarters as they had on the outside.

Just as she was summoning up the nerve to climb the steps and knock, she heard it again.

"Pauline! Over here!" It was the same young voice as before.

She turned her head in the direction she thought it came from. Nobody was there. Then, out stepped a boy from behind the apple tree.

It was Walter.

Her brother stood in the sunshine, smiling. He looked like he was posing for a photograph. In his left hand he clutched a half-eaten apple. In his right, he held Mark, his beloved tin soldier. He let both of them drop to the ground and broke into a run.

Pauline froze, a lump in her throat. She could only stand there as her brother, full of vitality, came barreling towards her. Gone was the pallor of the little boy who'd always been ill. Walter looked healthy and strong. His face was lit up with a smile that she had not seen in the last year or so of Walter's life; Poppa had wiped it from existence.

Walter ran into her with such a thud, he nearly knocked her down. She had to grab hold of him to keep her balance. Before she knew it, they were engaged in a humungous bear hug. Around and around they danced, in a giddy circle, squeezing the stuffing out of one another. Her laughter mingled with his in a joyful song that carried into the treetops.

Out of breath and dizzy, the two children stopped to catch their breath. Pauline stared at her little brother in disbelief. He was real! She'd felt his heartbeat against hers. This wasn't a mirage or a dream. She brushed away happy tears from her cheeks.

"I thought I'd never see you again," she said, sniffling and trying hard to regain her composure.

"We knew you'd come home before too long," Walter said knowingly.

"We?" Pauline asked.

Walter didn't say another word. He just grinned from ear to ear and looked back towards the house. Pauline followed his glance.

The door swung open. Pauline knew, even before she saw, that it would be Mama. Sure enough, her mother appeared on the top step. She was wearing her Sunday dress, and looked so beautiful, so young, that Pauline was struck speechless. Her legs felt like they were made of water when she tried to walk.

She didn't have to walk very far. Mama hurried down the steps and ran to her. After all the months she'd been deprived of her mother's loving touch, Pauline felt pure exhilaration as Mama embraced her. She closed her eyes and let herself be held, wrapping her arms gently around Mama's waist. A flood of memories washed over her: the smell of the gingerbread cookies Mama made at Christmastime, and of the pork roast she cooked on Easter Sunday. She recalled being four years old and laying her hands on Mama's belly, feeling her little brother kick inside the womb, and the proud look on Mama's face when Pauline learned to give him his bottle. She remembered lullabies sung, fairy tales told, and a million other wonderful things she'd long since forgotten.

Mama broke their embrace and with soft hands, tilted Pauline's tear-stained face upwards.

"There now, baby," she said. "What is there to cry

about?"

Pauline looked at her mother's pretty face, at the inviting house, and at Walter, who was perched contentedly on the branch of their apple tree.

"Nothing," she answered. "Everything is perfect now."

EPILOGUE

The Daily Journal

Thursday June 6, 1935

Wednesday was a day of tragedy and shock in the North Country, as fire, and a chance discovery, resulted in three deaths, most likely all in the same family.

At around 4:05AM, fire fighters were alerted by John P. Saunders, when he noticed smoke billowing from the tree tops in the woods, northeast of his farm on Driscoll Road. A fire truck arrived at the Willow Lane residence of William G. Frasier around 4:15, only to find it fully engulfed in flames. The firemen kept the blaze confined to the structure, and it was finally extinguished by 6AM. Mr. Frasier, 42 years old and an employee of the Kellogg Lumber Company, was found deceased in the ruins of his home. Although Mr. Frasier was thought to have lived alone, the burned remains of a female child were also discovered. It is assumed that the dead child is his daughter, Pauline M., aged 10, although a positive identity has yet to be made. Mr. Frasier had informed acquaintances that Pauline was with her mother, Mary R., whereabouts unknown. He had given contradicting accounts of his wife and daughter's location, but said that Mary had run off with another man, taking the child with her. This fact has never been corroborated, nor was it ever investigated. Mrs. Frasier and young Pauline had not been seen or heard from since sometime in March.

In a strange and shocking coincidence, a vagrant man, Alfred P. Jones, was looking for a place to spend the night, out of the terrible thunderstorm, when he came upon an abandoned shack. This structure is located alongside the railroad tracks, about a mile and a half South of the downtown station. Once inside, Mr. Jones discovered a badly decomposed corpse. He ran all the way to town, and reported his finding at the police station at around 3:50AM. Officers arrived on the scene less than half an hour later, and the body was removed. Some clothing still remained in tact, indicating that the remains were those of a woman. She was estimated to have been dead for 3 to 6 months. Oddly enough, records show that the shack where the woman's body was found was once owned by none other than the deceased William G. Frasier himself. He and his family lived there until 1931, when he inherited the Willow Lane house from his late father, Albert P. The speculation- which, for now is just that- is that Mary Frasier never left town at all, and that it is her body that was found by Mr. Jones. The late Mr. Frasier's penchant for alcohol and his violent temperament were well-known among those close to the family.

Even after the bodies have all been identified and buried, the full story of what happened to the Frasier family may never be known.

A son, Walter A., died of pneumonia this past January, at the age of 6.

LaVergne, TN USA
04 November 2009
163026LV00002B/32/A